GATES OF POWER

PETER O'MAHONEY

Gates of Power
Jack Valentine Book 1

Peter O'Mahoney

Copyright © 2020
Published by Roam Free Publishing.
peteromahoney.com

1st edition.
All rights reserved. No part of this publication may be reproduced, stored in a retrieval system, or transmitted, in any form or by any means without the prior permission in writing of the publisher. This is a work of fiction. Any resemblance to any person, living or dead, is purely coincidental.

Cover design by Belu.
https://belu.design
All rights reserved.

ALSO BY PETER O'MAHONEY

In the Jack Valentine Series:

Stolen Power

*****

In the Tex Hunter series:

Power and Justice
Faith and Justice
Corrupt Justice
Deadly Justice

*****

In the Bill Harvey Legal Thriller Series:

Redeeming Justice
Will of Justice
Fire and Justice
A Time for Justice
Truth and Justice

GATES OF POWER

JACK VALENTINE THRILLER BOOK 1

PETER O'MAHONEY

CHAPTER 1

A SCREAM more animal than human echoes through the narrow corridor. I run towards it, my mouth dry and chest heaving like a bellows.

Two gunshots.

The acrid smell of propellant fills the already suffocating air.

The screaming continues.

I power forward as paintings on the wall whizz past me in a blur: smiling faces with stick arms and giant fingers; rainbows, cotton clouds and big round lollipop suns; smiling parents and siblings. Happiness. Joy. Innocence. But it's pain that permeates the place today.

Unimaginable pain.

I round the corner and hell stretches before me. Small, fragile bodies lay strewn around a classroom. Hideous wounds. Blood smeared around like paint. The slaughter of the innocent. My eyes dart about, searching frantically.

And there she is: Claire; my Claire.

Choking. Gasping. Nearly breathless.

Dying on the floor, clutching the lifeless body of a

little boy as if he were her own son, the child we could never have. A wail erupts from the depths of her soul as she stares into my eyes, begging me for help, to take it all away, to wake her from this horrific nightmare.

Only it is me who wakes, screaming into the night, and guilt floods over me like the full, cold weight of the ocean.

Three years had passed since Claire's murder, since my heart was shattered into a thousand pieces with no way to put it back together. I'd locked it away securely but it haunted me at night, when my defenses were down. And the dream would recur.

He killed himself, of course. They always do. Robbing me of retribution and leaving a gaping Claire-shaped hole in my life that nothing could ever fill. I'd tried the bottle, prescription drugs, women; hell, I'd even tried the church, briefly. The only thing that quietened my demons was my work as a private investigator.

And so, I threw myself into it.

It's what you do: you continue, you keep fighting, keep trying to move forward, keep trying to honor their memory.

And a new case had just arrived, and it was one of my favorites: a murder investigation.

*****

This was not like Claire's funeral, more like a circus, and yet it still brought it all back.

Some people who knew Brian Gates turned up looking sincere, some were there to support loved ones, but the majority were there out of obligation. It was the public, those who only knew his television persona, that looked the most bereaved.

Still, that's not to say there was a shortage of women there to emotionally unburden themselves on the makeshift stage, highlighting their own 'special connection' with the deceased, each staking a claim to the top-spot in his affections: that it was her, and her alone, who really understood him, as he did her.

Truth was, he probably wouldn't remember any of their names.

As memorials go it was grandiose: Chicago's Cultural Center with its huge pillars and high domed ceiling, decked out with more flowers than a florists' convention—a perfect send-off for the famous or the infamous, and Brian Gates was both in equal measure. High above the stage hung a giant version of his cheesy publicity photo. There he was all fake tan and porcelain pearly whites, sitting on his famous TV studio desk, pointing a long index finger at the camera, thumb up, while winking and flashing that trademark toothy Cheshire cat grin.

A well-built African American man, television

producer Pat Packman, addressed the crowd, strutting back and forth across the stage. Microphone in hand, he was throwing his own brand of contrived smiles at those gathered below in a poor imitation of the man he eulogized. He looked like he loved being in front of the camera, but he lacked the charisma to work the crowd and his delivery was flat.

"He commented on politics daily but he was the most politically incorrect man I knew. And I say that as a compliment!"

Polite smiles were flashed from the public gallery.

"When my Netflix special on Brian Gates aired last June, it polarized people's opinions more than any other program I've produced. I think it's fair to say that women in particular were divided. Sure, there were those who considered him a chauvinist, a TV throwback to another era, but even his staunchest detractors would have to admit to Brian's undeniable charm. My favorite response to the program was from a woman who told me: 'If I'd have met Brian Gates, I may well have had an affair with the man, because he was self-confident and funny, but I would have hated myself for it in the morning.' As you know, this was far from a unique reaction."

The crowd laughed at this one, while a few of the celebrities smiled uncomfortably.

Everyone knew what he was referring to. When hosting a TV debate on gender rights and freedom of speech, Gates had drawn the anger of a leading feminist academic after repeatedly referring to her throughout the program as "Hun," and "Sweetie" before closing his argument with, "Sweetie, if I agreed with you, we'd both be wrong!" She hit the roof, but Gates played it cool. "The last thing I want to do is hurt you..." he replied with mock sincerity, "but it's still on the list of possibilities," he added, miming slapping her ass. There was an uproar in the studio, but a week later it came out in the press that after the show he'd worked his legendary charm, had taken her for a drink to smooth things over, and had ended up bedding her. After that her career was in tatters, but Brian Gates became a legend.

The Netflix special had introduced Gates to a whole new generation. A generation raised on rampant political correctness, but who, none-the-less, took him to heart, and soon referred to him affectionately as "The Gates." For many he became the refreshing antidote to the "snowflake social-justice-warriors" with their recreational outrage at the slightest political indiscretion. He became retro cool in that one-liner 70s male chauvinist pig sort of way and became the most unlikely of internet stars when a compilation of his greatest quips went super viral.

You know, like:

"Bigamy, the practice of marrying two wives, should be defined as having one wife too many. Monogamy should be described as the same."

"Taking a woman home involves math skills—you have to add the bed, subtract the clothes, and pray that you don't multiply."

Some, it's got to be said, were better than others. When reading a story about a baker with a gun, he concluded the piece with the now immortal words, "Go ahead. Bake my day."

That little nugget helped him land a gig as a judge on a panel for a series of bakery shows, until, that is, it came out that 'The Gates' had slept with two of the other three panelists: the famous celebrity chefs—and sisters—Anna and Clare McMann.

Yeah, Brian Gates was a character, alright.

His viral fame was somewhat ironic, he often got riled up about the malign influence of the internet, how it was making the youth of America fat and lazy with their virtual friends and virtual passions, playing virtual sports and living virtual lives.

But his real pet peeve were the gamers. And it was the biggest of them all who had been charged with his murder: Gaming superstar and poster boy, Alfie Rose.

I admit, it was an alien world to me—that people would pay good money to watch someone play 'shoot-'em-up' video games. But its popularity was undeniable, and Alfie Rose was huge. With millions of followers on Instagram, Facebook, Twitter, you name it, he was an all-around social media mega star with the looks to match. And by all accounts likable too. Sort of a modern rock star, a guy that young girls want to follow, and the boys want to be.

The bad blood between Rose and Gates started after Gates referred to Rose as a 'Mommy's basement loser boy' live on air. That was the spark that lit the fire. Soon they were trading regular insults on their respective platforms, and their devotees took it real serious.

I'd taken the call from Alfie Rose myself.

His trial began in two weeks and he was staring down a stretch inside of twenty plus years. Sure, his lawyers had hired private investigators, but he didn't trust them—his attorneys or the PIs—they'd been encouraging him to take a deal for 10 years. Floating the idea with a little too much enthusiasm, pushing him to take the plea, like they thought he'd done it. He was pleading not guilty, and wanted to prove as much, but it was too late now to jump ship and hire a new team, and, to be fair, the case against him was strong.

That's when my name came up. As it often does. I don't advertise but I'm never short of work.

If people want the best, then they know who to hire: Jack Valentine.

By now the man on stage was warmed up.

"I guess it's no secret that producers don't always like the stars they work with, but it would be hard not to like Brian Gates, he was an exceptional man. He was certainly not like the new generation of newscasters, with their clean-cut ways and phony outrages, politely tip-toeing around an issue so as not to offend. Not Brian, he liked to state the case for something in the most extreme terms with real conviction and belief. He was the last of a dying breed, and with his passing, the news reading world is a lot less fun, and I for one lament that, as I do the passing of a friend."

Packman wrapped up proceedings soon after, hitting "play" on a video of Gates' famous viral one-liners, which sprang to life on a screen behind the stage.

Before the applause subsided, I slipped outside.

If I had hoped to go unnoticed it wasn't meant to be. As I stood watching people leaving a familiar face approached: Hugh Guthrie, one of Brian's rival newscasters.

"Well, if it isn't Mr. Super Sleuth himself. Nice suit. Italian made?"

"I own a lot of nice suits, but I only bring this one out for funerals. I'll even wear it to yours; which will hopefully be sometime soon." I pulled at the collar of my shirt, loosening the tie that was trying to strangle me. "Good to see you've put partisan issues aside to be here, Hugh."

"You know what it's like with family events, you might not wanna go but you gotta go. If not, your absence is noted. And us newscasters are family."

"Touching, Hugh. Real touching."

Our paths had crossed many times before, most recently when Hugh hired me to dig up dirt on a rival to secure a job. Messy business, but he got the result he wanted. Did I like him? No, but that wasn't a prerequisite to me taking a case.

"I'd like to know what you do in the gym, Valentine. Your arms look thicker than my torso."

"You could pray for better genetics." I stepped towards him, engulfing him under my shadow. "Because nothing else is going to help you."

Truth was, I didn't work that hard in the gym. I had been blessed with the genetic lottery: I towered over most people, still had a full head of hair at forty, and every time I looked at the gym, my muscles seemed to grow.

"A little birdy told me you were looking into Gates' murder, Jack. I heard that the gamer gave you a call himself. Do you think he did it?" Always the reporter, Guthrie pushed for information.

"This is a funeral, Hugh. You should have left your reporter hat at home."

"I think a lot of people had a motive to kill the man. He made a lot of people angry along the way and pushed the buttons of powerful people. Sure, he had fans, people who idealized his persona, but behind closed doors, the guy was a walking time-bomb; no-one knew when the next scandal was going to break, all everyone knew was that there would always be one more."

"He left a trail of spurned lovers and angry husbands in his wake. No offense, Hugh."

"That's a long time ago. You know we patched up our differences, right?"

I didn't respond, as the person in question was already on her way over: Lizzie Guthrie, far younger than Hugh and a delicate woman—not delicate like a flower, delicate like an unexploded bomb.

"What a load of guff!" she spat out with the tenderness of a woman scorned. "I know it's not the right thing to speak ill of the dead, but that doesn't mean you have to practically canonize them. A good friend of his? Puh-lease! Everybody knew Packman couldn't stand him."

"The producer?" I asked.

"Yeah, Pat Packman. Hated Gates but made him very rich."

"Why'd he hate him?"

"Oh, you know, the usual with Gates." Lizzie's comment was flippant. "Packman's wife left him to be Gates' fourth."

"Still, they had an eminently successful working relationship," added Hugh. "And Packman couldn't ignore that. After all, it's called show business, not show friendship. Never underestimate the supreme power of the almighty buck."

"He had to pander to Gates' needs, mind you. There was only one star of that show and he expected to be treated accordingly. It must have driven Packman crazy, it would me," added Lizzie. "How could you work with the man that stole your wife?"

Hugh's face creased ever so slightly, and I caught a glimpse of the pain that still sat with him. It's all good and well to say that the past is the past, that all has been forgiven, but even someone as heartless as Hugh must've felt some residual pain after Lizzie cheated on him with none other than "the Gates" himself.

A stream of people started departing the hall,

mainly Joe Public, but then a familiar face emerged.

"Speak of the devil," said Hugh.

Striding with purpose was Pat Packman. Several paces behind but moving with the same urgency was a pale skinned woman with curly auburn hair, attractive but clearly agitated. I recognized her from the preliminary background checks I'd run on Gates: Kelly Holmes, the second wife.

A former model, she had married Brian when she was twenty-one and he was forty. She was forty-one herself now and had carved out a career as an actress on a daytime soap opera. Not the big time, but it was as far as she was going to climb.

"If anyone's got a motive it's her," quipped Lizzie. "The way he treated her. And all aired in public. Total humiliation. Rumor has it his girlfriend turned up on their honeymoon and when she protested, he told her, 'Darling, you should be more like the French. French men have girlfriends and mistresses, why can't you be like them?' By all accounts she was, for a while. But you can't put up with that forever, unless you're a doormat, and she proved otherwise. Good settlement in the end. Must have sweetened the pill. Especially given Gates was such a miser."

"So, what do you think, Valentine? Could one of them have done it?" asked Hugh. "Come on, Valentine, who do you think the guilty party is? The gamer or one of them?"

He made it sound like he was joking, like he wasn't really digging for information, but I could read him like a book, and it wasn't a good one. They could dig all they wanted; they weren't getting anything from me I didn't want them to get.

It was going to be a difficult investigation with all the media attention, and people like Guthrie weren't going to make it easy for me. They were in a feeding frenzy, hungry for more, and I didn't intend to supply them with cheap food.

But there was one thing I knew, one thing that was clear from the moment Alfie Rose called me: I was stepping into a dangerous world, and death was going to follow me.

CHAPTER 2

JAGGED SHARDS of glass explode from the window, showering the couch and carpet, shattering the midnight serenity in an instant. It's dark, barely enough light to see, but suddenly light is everywhere. Blinding light, as flames engulf the living room.

Fire sprints up the curtains, devouring their fabric in a heartbeat as they collapse to the floor limp and consumed; next goes the couch, thick, dark clouds billowing violently from its core as the inferno spreads at terrifying speed. In the corner of the room a dog awakes, panicked, running back and forth with no way to escape.

Suddenly, a figure appears, difficult to see amid the turmoil, holding something, there's another cloud, this time white as carbon dioxide fills the air, choking out the blaze, and mercifully the flames subside. The dog leaps into the figure's arms and as the smoke clears his face becomes apparent: Alfie Rose.

I clicked "stop" on the first of two video surveillance files that had landed in my inbox overnight.

The other one was less dramatic: an exterior view

of Alfie Rose's house with the two arsonists sprinting away towards a getaway vehicle.

The attack was over a week ago, and I guess in part, it prompted Rose's call to my office.

I took a long sip of coffee—double strength and black—and tried to focus. This was proving difficult as I could sense a presence in the corner of the room. You know, that feeling like you're being watched? That's how it felt. I glanced towards it for the umpteenth time: the pack of cigarettes on the table. Was I looking at it or was it looking at me? It sure felt like the latter. I'd been resisting all morning, badly. Claire had always badgered me to quit, but temptation was wearing me down.

"Oh, hell!" I cracked, headed over to the pack and lit one up, inhaling deeply.

A mixture of instant relief and guilt.

Nicotine for relief, guilt on account of Claire.

With a contrite apologetic smile, I looked towards an unlikely feature on the wall that reminded me of her: an antique mirror. We'd argued plenty about its location. I said it was too low to be practical for me to use without ducking. She said it wasn't her fault that I was six-foot-four, and that it needed to be low, so it matched the pictures on the wall and balanced the room. She'd won out. Now I wouldn't move it for the world, not that I thought she'd been right or anything, but in a small way it was a part of her, like most of the apartment really, which I'd kept the same since her murder.

To change it now would feel like erasing that tiny bit of her I had left.

Silly, I know. But there you go.

An interior design feature of a very different kind had spurred Alfie Rose to install video cameras at his place. Soon after he'd been charged with murder, in an ominous gesture of things to come, an intruder had left an ax embedded in the floor of his living room.

Alfie was out on bail now, set at a million dollars, and was required to turn over his passport due to his flight risk.

I'd spoken to him again on the phone this morning. He'd sounded panicked, and nervous, a far cry from the uber confident image he portrayed online. It was hardly surprising given that there had been a genuine real-world attempt on his life. The arson attack was part of the escalating threats, part of the swelling disgust the public had for him, and I loathed to think where things were going to end up.

The case was getting serious, and the constant stream of online abuse and threats from devoted fans of Brian Gates were increasing.

We'd arranged a meeting, our first, and he wanted it kept quiet.

His lawyers didn't know about me and he wanted to keep it that way. It wouldn't last for long, of course, not if others had already heard a whisper that I was on the case, but for now it served us both to keep it from them, lest they see my involvement as meddling in their affairs.

I was ready for some face to face time with Rose. I wanted to watch his reactions, get a feel for him as a person, and ask myself the big question: did I believe him?

I was familiar with the kid's background, what had been in the press anyway: twenty-two years old, a likable giant, loved for his smile and personality, and wild sense of fashion, he was highly intelligent but dyslexic and had struggled at school but excelled with computers. The school jocks had bullied him, but he got back at them in spectacular style when he hacked into the school yearbook page and edited his tormentors' entries with honest and witty appraisals, detailing their sadistic abuse of others and limited prospects when they finally graduated. He shared it far and wide and in no time, it went viral across the net. Three million likes on Facebook, with a hundred thousand corresponding comments, hundreds of thousands of retweets, front page of Buzzfeed; and plenty more besides.

That little stunt got him expelled but he had the last laugh. He became an internet star, and within the year had pulled in his first million as a gamer, purchased a bright fire-engine red convertible Ferrari and decided to pay his main former tormentor a little visit—at the drive-through where the guy now worked. Pulling up with the top down and three adoring female fans in the back, Rose coolly placed his order with the bully, then asked to speak to the manager. On arrival he handed the manager five grand in cash, 'paying it forward' for the next two hundred plus customers.

"Nice to see you, Chad. Good to see you're doing so well," remarked Rose, before wheel-spinning off into the sunset.

As I pulled up at a towering luxury apartment block in the city's exclusive West Loop district, the valet looked at me without warmth. I could see what he was thinking: "You want me to park that?"

In exchange for my beat-up old Chevy truck keys, I received the sort of look one might expect were you to drop a half-eaten sandwich into the palm of a stranger.

If he was expecting a tip, he forfeited it today.

I left him to it and headed inside.

Chandeliers, giant potted palms, and more marble than the Taj Mahal decked out the expansive lobby. 'Mommy's basement' it most certainly was not, and Alfie Rose had the best suite of them all, the penthouse.

After the arson attack on his house in Naperville, Illinois, around forty-five minutes from Chicago, Rose had moved into his downtown apartment.

It was the right move, given the added security, which proved effective at vetting me thoroughly at the concierge desk before green-lighting my ride to the top floor in the elevator.

The doors opened and there he stood. He was taller than I imagined, about six-foot-two and well turned out, good-looking, I guess, in an androgynous kind of way, with long curly hair and a well-kempt beard. Dressed in a combination of rock star meets lord of the manor attire, he looked like he'd come off a fashion show catwalk, sporting his trademark steampunk top hat complete with cooper aviator googles, a gentleman's waist coat and open-neck shirt combo, displaying several prayer beads and crucifixes. Skintight ripped jeans and cowboy boots finished the look.

Subtle he wasn't, but the girls were crazy about him.

"Thanks for coming, Mr. Valentine," he said, flashing a smile and shaking my hand, firm and strong. "Please, come in."

I stepped into an ultra-modern palace overlooking the city. Open-floor plan and the size of a couple of basketball courts, giant floor-to-ceiling glass walls framed it on every side, making it stretch out into the sky and providing a sprawling eagle's-eye view of the city. Strewn about among the collections of modern sculptures and artwork was every conceivable gadget, from miniature drone aircrafts to virtual reality headgear and gloves. Much of this I recognized, with the apartment serving as a suitably impressive backdrop to many of Rose's online videos and Instagram posts.

It was kind of interesting, if you like that sort of thing, but I was no real estate agent—thank God—and I sure wasn't here to sightsee.

We'd already exchanged pleasantries on the telephone, so I decided to skip the preamble and get down to business. After all, time was ticking.

"I'm going to run through the prosecution's case against you," I said, pulling out a chair to sit at the glass dining table. "Then I want to hear your version of events, every detail, understand?"

He nodded with the obedience of a drowning man thrown a lifeline, then pulled out a chair and settled in for my evaluation.

At first glance the prosecution's scenario appeared watertight: while at a star-studded charity event, the two arch rivals, Brian Gates and Alfie Rose, finally came face to face. Gates, who was presenting the second half of the event, proceeded to make Rose the butt of several jokes, which became more disparaging as the evening progressed.

Allegedly, when the evening came to a close, Rose followed Gates back to his dressing room to have it out with him. Here an argument took place which turned physical. Rose struck Gates, who fell, hit his head and then when he was unconscious, struck him with a fatal blow, this time to the temple with a champagne bottle, the resulting impact cracking Gates' skull.

In a panic, Rose tried to cover up the incident, but did so in an amateurish manner, moving the body and wiping blood from the chairs but not the carpet, before jettisoning the whole silly idea of concealing what had happened, fleeing with it only partially done.

As for witnesses, they confirmed that Rose had entered Gates' dressing room. And the material evidence was incriminating too, Gates' blood was discovered on Rose's clothing. Alfie Rose was arrested and charged with murder.

"Obviously, that's not the way it went down, Mr. Valentine," said Alfie, with a pained smile after hearing my summary. "But bits of it are true, just not the crucial bits."

"Take me back to the start," I said. "How did the evening begin?"

"It began with a charity auction, not hosted by Brian Gates but by a professional auctioneer, and the first item up for grabs was a bottle of champagne; just to get the event started, you know. Now I don't care too much for alcohol, but I threw in a bid or two for the fun of it, at which point Brian Gates realizes that I'm there too and starts bidding against me with a vengeance. Everyone knows there's a beef between us, so the other bidders drop out and leave us to it, so it's just Gates and me going head to head, for something I didn't really want in the first place."

"But by now the wheels were in motion, and you don't want to back down and lose face, right?" I said.

"Exactly. Anyway, the auctioneer was loving it, 'Do I have fifteen thousand? Fifteen bid. Do I have sixteen thousand? Sixteen bid. Seventeen?' On and on it went, up and up, the crowd egging us on, by the time it reached fifty thousand I think both of us were looking for an exit, but he didn't want to blink first.

At fifty-five I bowed out, as gracefully as I could. In that moment Brian Gates jumped to his feet and punched the air in triumph, until, I think, it dawned on him that Alfie Rose, of all people, had just made him pay fifty-five thousand dollars for a bottle that was probably worth a thousand."

"And rumor has it he was really tight," I said, poorly suppressing a smile.

"Yeah, they say he made scrooge look like a public benefactor," laughed Alfie. "So, no prizes for guessing who was the focus of his jokes when he took to the stage as presenter for the rest of the evening."

"And after the event, you admit that you went back to his dressing room?"

"Yeah, of course, but it wasn't to have it out with him. I wanted to smooth things over, bring an end to the constant jibes back and forth and to offer him a truce. Honestly, I've got better things to do with my time than perpetuate some pointless feud with a TV dinosaur. He lived in a different world than me, and his audience wasn't my audience, so I saw no point in continuing to argue. I went to his dressing room to see if we could put it all to rest."

"What was his response?"

"By this stage he'd been drinking all evening and was pretty hammered, but to my surprise, he agreed. He seemed a pretty happy drunk to me, not one of those down and depressed drunks that wants to fight, but the sort that loves everybody, and wants to let them know. I believe his words were, 'You know I love you really, Rosie-boy!' Then he put his arm around my shoulders and said, 'Take one of your selfie photos of us, together! Let's give them something to talk about!' So, I did, with both of us smiling for all the world to see. He then reached under a table and pulled out the bottle of champagne, all fifty- grand's worth, and says, 'Let's have a drink, come on, have a drink on me, Alfie!' We tried to toast each other but, like I said, the guy was drunk, and as he tried to clink his glass on mine, he broke it. That's when he cut his hand. I tried to stop the bleeding with a Kleenex, but it was gushing everywhere, not that he seemed that bothered, in fact, he kept laughing at my useless medical assistance. Anyway, that's how his blood got on my clothing."

I watched Rose closely as he told me this. His hands shook and he fought back tears as he talked, but who wouldn't be nervous given his situation? His world had been turned upside down—he'd gone from hero to zero in the matter of months, and the love that people had for him had been replaced by vile hatred. As a man that lived in his own cocooned world, he obviously never thought he'd have to deal with regular death threats, and yet, here he sat, having survived an arson attack.

Herd mentality had always been a social phenomenon, but the age of social media had turned it into a weapon. The keyboard warriors had focused their animosity towards Rose, and the herd quickly jumped onto the bandwagon. Under the effects of herd mentality, people are known to make highly emotional decisions, rather than rational ones, making different choices than they would individually. Gates had experienced a lot of love from the public before he died, and the feelings of loss, grief and anger had to be directed somewhere—unfortunately it was all aimed at the man who was claiming he was innocent.

Did I believe Rose had nothing to do with it? To be honest, I hadn't made up my mind yet.

"And you left after he cut his hand?" I asked.

"Yeah, after we stopped the bleeding by wrapping his hand in a cloth, I gave him my hat as a present, the same type as this one, to sort of commemorate our newfound friendship, and then I left."

"Did anyone see you leave?"

"Not that I'm aware of."

"And the photo, you posted this to social media at what time?"

"10:30pm, but the police won't consider this as evidence. His body wasn't found until the next morning and they're estimating the time of his death as 11pm."

"So, their reason being: no big deal, you just killed him after taking the photo?"

He nodded, glumly this time.

"Do you think you can help me?" he asked, a marked degree of concern registering on his face. "I've hired the best defense team money can buy, but, like I said on the phone, they're pushing for me to take the deal. It feels like they're more concerned with not losing a case, rather than keeping me out of prison. And even if I switch at this late stage, I doubt I'll get a better team, only more of the same with even less time to prep. I'm sure they don't want to take this case to trial."

"You won't take the deal for ten years?"

"No way," he said, shaking his head in despair. "I won't survive that. I know I won't. School was a hideous prison for me, and I'm not going to a literal, infinitely worse version. At least not without a fight. I have to do everything I can to prove my innocence."

I admired the kid's spirit, but the way events were unfolding, he would be lucky to make it to his trial date.

I didn't tell him this, but he knew it well enough. The crazies were out there screaming for blood, the obsessive Brian Gates fans who had pronounced him guilty as charged and would love to put him six feet under.

The question was: could I solve the case before they succeeded?

CHAPTER 3

IF YOUR resume includes getting fired for arguing with a colleague during live-on-air news crosses, then chances are you won't get another interview for a job, let alone an actual job, with a serious news agency. But if you also had a physical altercation with the same colleague, then I'd say your chances are zilch.

So why did I hire Casey May as my assistant?

In a word: character. I respected that more than social niceties. And the way I saw it, there had been extenuating circumstances.

A college dropout, she had found a job in the mailroom of News Incorporated, where she proceeded to work her way up, landing a gig as a feature writer for one of their magazines, but eventually the role of deputy editor—their youngest ever at the time. From there she moved to the television division as part of an investigative journalism team, then scored a role in front of the camera as an on-the-ground reporter.

For someone whom the word 'sassy' could have been minted, it was a risky move.

It wasn't that she couldn't take criticism, but she didn't take BS from anyone: male or female, young or old, higher up the corporate chain or lower down, behind the camera or in front of it. It didn't matter to Casey, if you didn't treat her with respect then she was going to call you out on it, sometimes in spectacular style, regardless of the consequences.

At first her move into television had gone swimmingly, a successful career as a reporter punctuated by a couple of minor awards for investigative journalism—and a couple of major ones narrowly missed—she was definitely going places and was getting noticed by all the bigwigs at the station, and for the right reasons.

Not that it was all high-brow investigative content that garnered people's attention, she once was named in a poll that became the source of much tongue-in-check amusement to her, and her former work colleagues: an online vote to find Chicago's Top 10 Hottest News Reporters. Yeah, it's fair to say, that for a while, "Number Nine's" brand was on the rise

But then she reported on an upgrade to municipal cycle lanes—sometimes it's a slow news day and you gotta go where the producers send you—and things fell apart faster than cheap particle board furniture left in the rain.

She asked a woman on one side of the argument her opinion then turned to a man on the opposite side of the issue for his. A couple of bland responses and it was time to wrap things up, with her allocated timeframe almost at an end. A quick "thank you," a "back to the studio," and Casey's work was done.

Or so she thought.

But the female anchor wanted more.

"Is that it?" the anchor remarked with marked condescension. "I'd like to hear more from the woman. She made an interesting point. I'd like to hear her elaborate on it. Ask her about it."

By this stage the woman had walked off.

"She's departed, I'm afraid," replied Casey, doing her best to keep it professional.

But the anchor wouldn't let it go.

"Well, that's a shame, you really should have dug a little deeper. That was poorly executed."

"Sounds like you're telling me how to do my job, Jessica."

"Well perhaps I need to. Maybe I should give you some lessons."

"Maybe you need some lessons on how to conduct yourself professionally. What's the matter, have you been hitting the wine again? It wouldn't be a first for you this early in the morning, would it?"

By this stage the producers were screaming in Casey's earpiece to shut up.

For a second the anchor was dumbfounded, left open mouthed after being comprehensively "owned like a boss" on air by a subordinate.

"Wow… err… well… it will be interesting to see if you've got the guts to say that to me in person."

"Happily. And then I'll wipe that fake tan right off

you afterwards!"

The producers cut away to a commercial break, but the damage was done.

And the worst was yet to come.

When Casey got back to the studio, the anchor confronted her; verbal sparks flew, but then the anchor made a big mistake: she took a swing at Casey—it was a very bad move indeed, given that Casey happened to be a former amateur boxer of some repute. A quick sidestep to evade the blow and a lightning fast counter to the gut saw her attacker drop quicker than the Dow Jones during a market crash.

It didn't matter that the anchor swung first, security marched Casey from the premises, and her media career was over.

I had first met Casey through her investigative journalism when she approached me for advice on bugging devices. We just clicked. I liked her no-nonsense way of dealing with things, and that she didn't take herself too seriously. After she was fired, she was on the lookout for work. I happened to need an assistant, and the rest is history.

Casey stepped into the cool, dark recesses of the Angry Friar a little after noon, squinting after the blinding midday light outside. The city was warming up, summer was upon us and my favorite subterranean bar was the perfect place to rendezvous away from the heat.

I spotted her before she did me. I normally

propped up the bar but was eating today, so had taken a booth. God knows how many years had passed since smoking was prohibited, but somehow the upholstery still smelled of tobacco. And the décor hadn't changed since long before that. The place was more shabby than chic, but the food was good, at least by my standards, which generally meant it was meat based and plentiful.

She spotted me and headed over, a large file under one arm.

"There you go, Valentine," she announced, dropping the file on the table and sliding into the seat opposite. "Urgh!" she exclaimed, recoiling in disgust on spotting my lunch. "You eat that garbage?"

"What's wrong with it?"

"Oh, I don't know, maybe you could try having some greenery once in a while, a vegetable wouldn't kill you."

"Last time I checked a potato was a vegetable."

"Those are French fries."

"Your point being?"

She shook her head.

"If you ever accepted my invitation, you'd know what a good home cooked meal was."

I smiled. She had a point.

"So, what have you got for me?" I asked.

She opened the file.

"Everything you ever wanted to know on Alfie Rose. Other than whether or not he did it, of course."

"You haven't included that? Come on, what am I

paying you for?"

She laughed, "Generally, to do the things you're incapable of, Valentine, which, let's be honest, is a big list."

"Yep, got no argument with that one," I replied.

"Did you hear Alfie's cars got vandalized?" she asked, getting down to business.

"Yeah, he called me after it happened. Sounds more panicked by the day. One was spray painted: 'Murderer gonna die,' in big red letters. What is it with these people? I get it that Brian Gates was popular, but some of his fans are just nuts."

"Gates was a key figure in the culture wars, speaking out against new wave feminism, against using gender neutral pronouns, you know, that sort of thing, which got him a big following among the 'alt-right.' And among them are some serious loons—boys that are disillusioned with the world, and want to go back to the 50s way of living, where they could do with women whatever they wanted."

"And now these loons are holding Gates up as some sort of martyr."

"Which is exactly what they were looking for." Casey shook her head. "A popular idol to back their cause. I imagine that he's going to be one of these people that become even more popular after their death, and I have a feeling that this is going to turn from a snowball into an avalanche. These people now have a voice."

"Which means we're gonna have to work fast on

this one. Trial date isn't the issue, it's life expectancy. When this much testosterone is involved, men can do stupid things. Trust me, I know. And at this rate, Rose will be lucky to see the end of the month. He's got a target on his back, and these boys all own guns."

Steve, the gruff bartender, waiter and occasional bouncer all rolled into one, with a face like a bulldog chewing a wasp, came over.

"What can I get you, ma'am?"

"Got any organic quinoa salads on the menu?"

He looked at her for a moment, the cogs in his head slowly turning, then looked at me, shrugged his shoulders and went back to the bar. Casey wasn't much of a pub grub sort of gal.

"So, who have we got in the frame?" asked Casey, barely missing a beat.

"Let's look at motive. And opportunity. Who not only had cause, but was present that night at the charity event? And who not only had motive to punch or push over the guy, but to strike him with a fatal blow with a champagne magnum? If it was just a punch or push then it could have been someone who, in the heat of the moment, snapped and lashed out without the intention to kill, but the bottle adds a whole new dimension. The pathology report says Gates sustained a serious secondary blow to the back of the head when he fell after being punched or pushed over, and then, presumably when on the ground, he sustained a fatal blow with the bottle to the temple."

"Messy business, I imagine."

I nodded and drew up my shortlist. "For me, two people stand out: Pat Packman and Kelly Holmes. Video surveillance shows them at the event, although the camera near Gates' dressing room was down that night."

"Word on the street is that Packman never got over his wife leaving him to be Gates' fourth squeeze. As I hear it, there wasn't a nice ending between Packman and his wife either," said Casey. "Must have been a constant thorn in his side working with Gates after that one."

"Can you imagine it, not only seeing Gates every day at work, but then having to interact with him and the wife that used to be his but was now Gates' at all those hideous work functions? Sure would drive me crazy. Can't blame the man for hating him, wanting him dead, even."

"And apparently, it was well known the two hated each other."

"Which brings us nicely to Kelly Holmes, Brian's second wife, that's a long-held festering hurt if ever there was one."

"Somewhat publicly displayed, too," added Casey with a wry smile, ever the master of the understatement. "If anyone was vocal about their hatred of Brian Gates it was her—of all the years of her life she wasted, her best years, his constant infidelity, how he used her like a piece of meat—which might make you wonder why on earth she was in attendance at his memorial?" she added, raising an eyebrow suggestively.

"I had been wondering that, but by the looks of it you're about to tell me. What have you dug up?"

"She became, and remains, very close to Gates' elderly mother, Winifred, nursing her through cancer years ago. The two bonded, not only over this, but their mutual frustration with Gates. His mother is a devout Catholic, and word is, that behind closed doors she too was very vocal about Gates' wayward lifestyle. It was out of respect for Winifred that Kelly Holmes attended his memorial."

"Interesting, didn't do her image any harm either: jilted lover shows her class in selfless magnanimous act. A sort of 'he went low, but I've gone high.'"

"You know I watched one of her shows yesterday as research," said Casey, rolling her eyes. "That's an hour of my life I'll never get back."

"Good to see you doing the hard yards there, partner."

"She played an action-hero's mother."

"How was she?"

Casey rapped her knuckles on the table, "About as wooden as this. But what she lacks in talent she more than makes up for in bra size and make-up. Which is, of course, just as important on the casting couch."

I laughed. "Well, she was definitely the person most open about their hatred of Gates, the public may have laughed it off as a lovers' tiff, but I want to know if there's more to it than that. And if Gates was as drunk as Alfie says, it wouldn't be impossible for a slight woman like her to topple him. Might be a good time for me to became better acquainted with Mrs. Kelly Holmes."

"I think you might be right," said Casey.

The question was, how?

CHAPTER 4

"HERE'S A good one for you, Jack. This will cheer you up," said Casey, as we walked out of the bar and into the fresh Chicago air. "A guy goes to the dog-pound and says, 'I want a blind dog for my mother-in-law.' 'A blind dog?' replies the man, 'Don't you mean a guide dog?' 'No,' he says, 'If it sees what she looks like, it'll go for her throat!'"

I laughed.

"Here's another one," said Casey, barely pausing for breath, impressed with her own comedic abilities. "I was at the bar the other night and saw six men kicking and punching my mother-in-law. The barman turned to me and said, 'Aren't you going to help?' 'No,' I said, 'six should be enough.'"

I laughed again. Then sighed. There weren't many things that left me with a deep feeling of foreboding, but a visit to my mother-in-law was one of them. And no amount of jokes was going to change that.

She'd requested I come out to see her, most likely out of her desire to inflict more pain on my life. We'd not been in touch for a couple of years, but I guess she figured she was entitled to a visit every now and again.

It wasn't that I didn't like the woman, you understand, only that being with her was hard work, she was opinionated. But at nearly eighty-years-old, I guess she had earned that right. Still, she was Claire's mother, so I owed her the respect that she deserved.

It had, of course, come at the worst possible time. I wanted to give my sole attention to the case, to helping Alfie, and answering the ultimate question: who really killed Brian Gates? There were several lines of inquiry I needed to follow up on, and these really couldn't wait.

Pat Packman needed looking into a lot closer, and with a degree of urgency. His motive looked stronger than anyone's, and when considered alongside the apparent fight he'd had with the deceased in the bathroom at the Charity event—well, let's just say he was a person of significant interest.

When she called that morning, I'd tried to explain to my mother-in-law how pressed for time I was, how I really couldn't come out to see her, that perhaps in a month or two's time would be better, but she was insistent.

I dug my heels in and said no.

But then she pulled out her trump card.

"I need to speak to you, and it relates to Claire."

It was all she needed to say.

And so, of course, I agreed to drop on by.

"Good luck, big guy." Casey playfully punched me on the arm. "If you can handle the worst this city has to offer, then I'm sure you can handle her."

I offered Casey half a smile.

Truth was, the worst this city had was violence, something I had become well versed in, but seeing my mother-in-law was a trip soaked in emotion, something I tried to avoid at all costs.

I drove slowly to the suburb where she lived, taking the longer scenic route, in an attempt to delay the unavoidable. She lived about 30 miles from Chicago in the suburban city of Wheaton, which was a nice place to come from… but not a good one to visit. I never liked it there, mainly through association: whenever I was in Wheaton it was on an in-law visit, which did a pretty good job of clouding my opinion of the place.

As I pulled my car up outside her traditional white clapboard house, with its neatly pruned and orderly yard, I was greeted by a familiar site: a giant Stars and Stripes fluttering majestically in the wind on a towering pole.

I sat in the car for a moment and just watched it rustle, stalling the inevitable.

It was a quiet street; the sort of place where young adults dream of bringing up their families. There were no front fences, kid's bikes were left in front yards, and basketball hoops were hung above the garages. I spotted a football being thrown across the street, from one side to the other, and the kids looked no older than twelve. I was about to warn them not to step on the grass in front of Laura's house, but with

Laura's hostility, I'm sure they already knew that.

Finally, I decided to man up and face the music.

With a deep foreboding breath, I opened the door of my car and stepped outside.

And then, as if on cue, she appeared. Stepping out from the shadows on the veranda, she came into the light, staring down at me below with a look of indifference. She always reminded me of a grumpy nun ready to wrap me over the knuckles with a wooden ruler at the slightest indiscretion, and today was no different.

"Laura, good to see you. You're looking well," I said, lying through my teeth on both counts, as I strode up the veranda steps to meet her.

"I do not look well. My skin is like a leather handbag, I have more wrinkles than a pug dog, and I've shrunk so much that I could fit into the clothes of a ten-year-old."

"Right. Well, the flag looks nice," I added, just making conversation.

"Of course, it does," she snapped. "If you're going to fly the flag then at least have the decency to fly one in Grade-A condition. Hardly American pride if it's tattered and torn or faded, now is it? I've had to make several complaints about the state of others' in the neighborhood. When a flag is so tattered that it is no longer fit to serve as a symbol of the United States, then it should be replaced and hung in a dignified manner. The flag represents a living country, Jack, and is itself considered a living thing."

"Well, yes. Err, I agree."

"I've just brewed some coffee," she said, opening the front door.

I stepped inside, and in doing so entered a dated homage to some indefinable period in the distant past when bad décor must have been a thing, and 'musty' was the aroma of choice.

It was just how I remembered it: crocheted blankets and doilies, decorative plates on the wall, sentimental chocolate box artwork, and a profusion of floral patterns throughout.

She fetched the coffee from the stove, poured it methodically into little patterned cups, then sat down with me at a kitchen table covered in a chintzy cloth protected with a clear wipe-clean plastic sheet.

"I saw you on the television the other month," she said, unimpressed.

"At the truck-stop incident?"

"Someone was throwing a bottle at you. You must have annoyed them?"

I laughed. "Casey mentioned that I'd made a fleeting appearance. They weren't throwing it at me, by the way; just worked out that way, bad aim and all that."

"You're still with that girl then?" she asked with an air of suspicion.

"We work together, Laura. That's all it's ever been or will be."

"Mmm," she replied, looking at me over the top of her spectacles. "I saw that Guthrie man on the television too, crawled out from under a rock, no doubt. It will never cease to amaze me that he won an award for that so-called documentary. Sensationalist and exploitative nonsense, more like it. Edited the footage of me to look and sound like a fool. He thought he was going to be the new Michael Moore for that thing, and nobody watched it."

I knew she'd bring up Hugh, but I didn't think it would be this quickly. That she hated him was a given, he'd presented a documentary on the school shooting that Claire and many others had died in. I didn't hate him for it, it was news after all.

That it was news only so briefly seemed tragic to me. It had changed my life forever, more than I could ever explain, but with mass shooting after mass shooting, it had been forgotten about quickly, as just one of many, a footnote in a long list of tragedies that were spreading across the country like an unchecked cancer.

But Laura didn't see it that way.

Guthrie had interviewed some of the victims' families and she was one of them. She hadn't come across very well on film, she'd appeared cold and detached, but for her it was a coping mechanism. She'd had a hard life and was a hard woman, not the sort of person to blab on emotionally because a camera was stuck in her face. But I knew Claire's murder had torn her world apart.

She was right about nobody seeing Guthrie's film though, obscure award or not, it barely made a blip.

"I ran into Hugh Guthrie as well. I was researching a new case, and there he was, still as creepy and sleazy as ever."

"I hope you punched him in the mouth."

"I was certainly tempted."

She paused for a moment, as if she was trying to find the right time to tell me something, but then shook her head. "You're working on a new case?"

"Yeah, that's right. I'm looking into the defense of Alfie Rose. He's hired me to investigate the circumstances of his arrest, looking to see if there's anything that everyone else has overlooked."

"He's the kid that killed the television newsman?"

"Brian Gates."

"Yes, of course; that's what the television said, his house was set alight for murdering the newsman."

"Allegedly murdering," I interjected. "And Alfie himself was nearly killed in that fire."

"Well, I can't say I liked that Gates fellow anyway. Bit full of himself, you know. Funny mustache too. But then, I suppose he did have a very public affair with Guthrie's wife, so he can't be all bad, hopefully it caused Guthrie a great deal of embarrassment and distress; horrible little man that he is."

"To be fair, Laura, I imagine there aren't many people you do like on the television."

"Not true," she stated with conviction. "I like that Chef Ramsey."

"Who?"

"Chef Gordon Ramsey. Englishman, swears at

people in their restaurants after eating their repulsive food. Compelling viewing. Have you not seen it?"

"Err, no Laura. Can't say I have."

"He's a man who speaks his mind and doesn't suffer fools gladly. He tells it the way it is, and makes no mistake. Yes, I like him. He doesn't do the news, though. Pity."

"Err, yes."

She took a long sip of coffee.

"I'll be dead within the next few months, Jack," she said calmly, as if discussing the weather.

"What?"

"It's cancer. In my lungs, in my liver, in my kidneys. Spreading everywhere. Nothing the doctors can do."

"Laura, that's awful. I'm so sorry…"

"You can drop the sentimentality. It's too late for that. This old gal is going to meet her maker, and make no mistake. It's going to happen soon enough, and no amount of sentiment is gonna stop that. My time has come."

"How long have you known?"

"Three weeks. I got the diagnosis on my birthday."

"That's terrible."

"Yep," she replied slowly, her voice bitter and breaking.

For a second, I thought she might cry.

But Laura Cooper was made of strong stuff and held it together, just.

"Is there anything I can do?" I asked.

"Everybody asks me that. And to everybody I say the same thing: no!" She paused, then fixed me with a steely stare. "But then you're not everybody, Jack; are you? And there is something you can do."

"Anything, Laura. Name it."

"I want justice for my Claire. Justice for our Claire."

"How?"

"That subhuman Alexander Logan got away with killing her and all those little children by blowing out his own brains, but what about the person who gave him the weapon, the person who gave a mentally unstable fifteen-year-old boy a firearm. We all know someone did that; you, me, the police. He had no access to a weapon, and suddenly, there he was with an unregistered gun. That's not coincidence, someone gave him that weapon. Someone gave him the opportunity to murder those people. But we still don't know who. I want you to find out. I want you to bring them to justice. Promise me that you'll do that, Jack. Promise this dying woman that you'll get justice for Claire."

"Laura, you know there's nothing I'd like more, but all leads went nowhere. The police and I looked into this, and we came up with nothing; whoever it was is a ghost."

"Well, maybe you didn't look hard enough. Don't just give up on a job half done. We may not have seen eye to eye over the years, you and me, but I always thought the man Claire married was a fighter. A fighter doesn't give up until the final bell rings. Go back to it, Jack. Go back and find justice for my daughter."

She folded her arms and sat back in her chair as if the conversation was finished, as if counsel had been given and there was nothing more she wanted to add.

What could I possibly do?

The woman was practically on her deathbed and was pleading with me for help.

But could I help? I really didn't think so.

I'd looked into this years ago and had hit a brick wall. I understood her frustration as a bystander not directly involved in the investigation on the ground, but frustration didn't solve cases, evidence did. And evidence was thin on the ground even back then.

As I was pondering this and my response to her, she did something unexpected and out of character: she reached forward and tenderly held my hand.

She looked into my eyes.

"Please," she whispered, tightening her fragile grip.

I looked back at her and for a moment saw the similarity between her eyes and Claire's. With my other hand I held onto hers too.

"Okay, Laura," I said, "I'll do it. I can't promise you that I'll succeed, but I promise you that I'll go back to it and try."

And with that she smiled.

CHAPTER 5

PEOPLE FOLLOW routines.

And the more they follow routines the less aware they are. The commonplace becomes the least observed. Watch tourists in a new location, they look at everything around them; it's fresh, new, captivating. Watch locals, and you'll notice a sort of tunnel vision of familiarity as their norm; they see less, observe less, and see the same things in the same way.

As surveillance targets go, today's was proving very unaware, the rut of routine having dulled their senses to almost null and void. There was little chance they would spot me, but I took precautions nonetheless: never giving my sole attention to anything, so as not to become fixated on the target at the expense of everything else, where I might, for instance, miss someone putting a tail on me; and carrying out my surveillance in that sweet spot where I was close enough to observe but far enough away not to be alert. People rarely have the capacity or inclination to monitor things a long way away from them, so it's a good idea to dwell there when tailing a moving target. That was fine for now, but today's target would require something a lot more up close and personal, at least later on, to obtain the sort of information I required.

By now it was late afternoon and I'd been following Kelly Holmes for the last three hours. She'd had her nails done, been to the gym, and met a male friend for coffee. It wasn't the most stimulating way to spend my day but tailing someone could have its moments. If it was a difficult target, I'd enlist several trusted operatives, back up for me and Casey, which could then be switched when necessary, so if the target proved aware, they didn't clock the same ugly mugs in every location they went. And ditto the above for vehicles, with us using several to minimize the chances of detection. But today I was working solo. I wanted to converse with Kelly Holmes alone, to strike up a conversation as if I was a random stranger, and I had a plan.

Casey had discovered Kelly's credit card statements the night before after a bit of late-night dumpster diving, providing us with a wealth of information. Casey had drawn the short straw with that task, but she had her own trademark solution to the smell: a dust mask smeared with copious quantities of Vicks. The credit card statements had given us details of an online dating site Kelly Holmes used. I say 'dating site,' but high-end casual liaison site would be more accurate, if the website's promo material was anything to go by. Being a minor public figure, she had obscured her profile so the fanboys wouldn't know it was her, but if you knew what you were looking for, it was easy enough to find.

Casey had set up a fake account with Kelly Holmes' perfect suitor and arranged a date: tonight, at a piano and jazz bar, Lazy Joes. Only Mr. Perfect was going to stand her up and I'd be there waiting to take his place.

Framed photos lined the softly lit deep red walls of the entrance hall, all the big names of the jazz and blues scene who had played here over the years, a nod to the pedigree of the venue, letting you know from the moment you stepped inside that this was no modern version of retro cool, but authenticity itself. History had taken place here and was embedded in the building's fabric. Beyond the hall sat the main arena, intimately sized with plush red seating and tables covered with freshly pressed cloths, polished wine glasses and decorative candle lighting. The place oozed glamour, and tonight's clientele, who were now slowly arriving, were dressed to match.

I arrived purposefully before Kelly Holmes and took a seat at the cocktail bar. I'd made her reservation with tonight's fake date at the adjacent table, so I picked up the drink menu and settled in. Several paragraphs waxing lyrical about the abilities of the bar's resident mixologists and their trademark inventions, and finally I found what I was looking for: the whiskeys.

Double shot on the rocks of Ireland's finest while I waited for her arrival.

And waited.

And waited some more.

Three whiskeys later and with the full set of a jazz combo on stage, and I was beginning to wonder if it was her who was going to stand me up, when, finally, she walked on in.

Dressed to the nines in a tightly fitting little-black-dress that left little to the imagination and highlighted her alabaster pale skin, she cut a mighty fine form for a woman in her mid-forties. It may have been two decades since her modelling career, but her high cheekbones, curly auburn hair and hourglass figure still had the heads turning as she strolled with poise and presence to her seat.

She'd kept me waiting, and I decided to do the same to her, not as payback, but so I could observe her reactions while in a state of disengagement, taking note of her unconscious body language. And it was body language that was going to give me the best indicator of truthfulness or deception on her part.

A direct link exists between our emotions and our physiology, so during those brief moments of increased stress when lying, our true emotions leak out through our gestures, gaze and posture. But to read these effectively you have to establish someone's baseline 'normal' behavior, and then note any deviations. I wanted to establish Kelly Holmes' baseline, observe what gestures occurred during stress, then see if those same gestures cropped up, even fleetingly, when we conversed. In this way, I could gauge if she was lying.

As the minutes ticked by, I watched her composure slowly slip away. The tell-tale checking of her phone, ample mojito refills, and subtle squirming in her seat spoke of her growing frustration at Mr. Perfect's no show. This was not a woman used to being stood up, at least not since her divorce to Gates. I'd read a couple of her post marriage interviews where she'd proudly boasted of becoming a strong, confident woman whom no man would ever walk all over again.

I texted a message from Mr. Perfect: Stuck in traffic. See you in ten.

She began tapping the edge of her phone on the table.

One. Two. Three. Four. Five taps.

Then she put it down flat.

I sat back and watched the pressure cooker build, the annoyance slowly spreading across her face, as ten minutes became twenty, and twenty became half an hour. I could have entered the fray sooner, brought her frustration to an end with my approach, but I took my time, while pondering the ever-present question on my mind: could she be the killer?

I texted again: Nearly there. Only ten minutes away.

She did the frustrated tapping routine and began pursing her lips.

Sound underhanded and manipulative? For sure, but my client was facing a solid twenty plus in the joint for murder, so there was no room for niceties. Kelly Holmes was a suspect, plain and simple. My priority was the case and Alfie Rose. Not the enjoyment or mockery of a Z-list celebrity on a night out listening to jazz and looking for casual love.

With an impatient click of her finger, she demanded the bill from the waitress.

As she got up to leave, I made my move.

"Seaside Postcards," I said flatly, looking her in the eye as she came within earshot.

She stopped dead in her tracks.

"Best darn performance I ever saw from a newcomer on Broadway."

"You saw it?" she asked, taken aback. "That was over fifteen years ago."

"Twice in one week. Spellbinding."

I stood up from the bar stool and reached out a hand, "Jack Valentine. Theater critic, in a former life."

"Err, Hi, Kelly Holmes, Broadway actress, in a former life."

Yeah, in case you're wondering, I was lying about the theater critic bit. I'd had a colorful past before becoming a PI, but of the many gigs I'd tried my hand at, theater critic wasn't one of them.

It was a set up.

Casey had done some digging and found out that Kelly Holmes' proudest work, and the only work she'd ever received a modicum of critical acclaim for, was her one and only part in an obscure Broadway production of Seaside Postcards. Other than that, her work had been panned, and rightly so.

She had quit the Broadway role after Gates' affair with the wife and two daughters of a Congressman hit the headlines. She never got another gig on Broadway and her career became a series of meaningless bit parts in daytime soap operas. If she had wanted to be considered a serious actress, then it hadn't happened. Her fate was forever to be defined instead as one of three things: wife of Brian Gates, ex-wife of Brian Gates, and now ex-wife of the late Brian Gates.

But tonight, I was defining her the way she always yearned for. She took the bait, and soon we had settled in at a table together and were embroiled in her favorite subject: Kelly Holmes. I indulged her ego, bestowing her with searching questions as to the interpretation of her Broadway character and motivation for the role.

A painful hour of contrived, pretentious guff in response, about her latent desires to communicate and reflect something powerful back to the audience, and I eventually turned the subject to Gates.

She was several drinks in by now and happily unburdening herself.

"Brian liked to see himself as a Peter Pan-like figure, you know, the boy who never grew up, young at heart, a seeker of escapism, and all that. And in a sense, he was like Peter Pan. Only not in the way he thought."

"What do you mean?"

"Did you know that the original Peter Pan was

devious and heartless; sadistic; evil, even. And a killer. All that Disneyfication that happened later is a far cry from the character J.M Barrie first dreamed up. Brian Gates might not have been a killer, but he was all of the rest, and plenty more besides."

She took a big swig of cognac.

"Don't ever believe the happy-go-lucky media version of the man. The real Brian Gates was one almighty son-of-a-bitch."

"Are you following his case?" I asked.

"Isn't everyone?"

"What do you make of the gamer, do you think he did it?"

"I don't know, maybe. But Brian was hated, viscerally hated, by a lot of people. Sure, a lot of idiots loved him in equal measure, but they never knew him. It could have been one of hundreds of jilted husbands whose wives Brian seduced."

"What about that producer of his, didn't his wife leave him to be Gates' fourth? Packman, something… Pat Packman. Yeah, that's it, you think it could have been him?"

For a split-second, I thought I saw a micro-expression of panic flash across her face, followed by its quick suppression.

"No. Not a chance. Not Packman. That was years ago. The two worked together, had a good relationship, in fact," she said, not once breaking eye contact with me.

"You ever meet him?"

She picked up her phone and tapped it on the table while pursing her lips, in the exact same manner as earlier.

One. Two. Three. Four. Five taps.

"Couple of times, I think," she replied, again not once breaking eye contact.

That she unnaturally held my gaze was interesting.

It's a common misconception that people don't hold eye contact when they lie. Not so. Eye contact is broken all the time during conversation, with our eyes darting about in all directions to better access information.

But so ingrained is the false belief that people don't hold eye contact when they're lying, that often people do the exact opposite, firmly holding your gaze while telling a lie in the belief they'll appear trustworthy. The incongruence of her gaze, and the reappearance of her phone tapping pursed-lipped stress gesture, left me certain she was lying.

But about which part?

I already knew that Packman hated Gates, but why lie about that and to what end?

Or maybe she was lying about Packman not being the killer. If so, what did she know?

Or was it that she was more familiar with Packman than she was letting on?

I plied her with more questions and a couple more drinks to try to find out, but she proved unyielding, as if a defense mechanism had kicked in after the mention of Packman's name, which only convinced me more than ever that there was something she was concealing.

She turned the conversation to trivial matters, and soon after began overtly demonstrating her availability: little head tosses, playing with her hair, gentle touches of my hand, and confident smiles followed by slow looks away.

They were all too easy to read. But that was intended.

As she finished her drink, she turned to me with amorous, bedroom eyes.

"Are we getting out of here?"

"We are," I stated without warmth. "Only it's in separate taxis."

CHAPTER 6

THE MOST essential stage of any private investigation work isn't the examination of the scene, the interviewing of witnesses, or the review of circumstances surrounding the incident. Nope. The most essential step, the one that often gives away the most information, is the collection of information about the person hiring the investigator.

Ordinary, regular people with ordinary, regular lives don't hire private investigators. People who are in trouble, people who have messed up, hire investigators. And more often than not, they're hiding something.

Alfie Rose grew up in the neighborhood of Logan Square, on the Northwest side of Chicago, and a lot of his classmates still resided there. The area was currently undergoing gentrification, but it still had its suspect characters, drugs, and criminal activity. Late night bars sat next to Mom-and-Pop shops, coffee shops were next to cheap defense lawyer's offices, and the upscale car yards were only a block from where a lot of homeless slept. I'd had a lot of work in the suburb over the years and knew the local characters well enough to go hunting for information.

Over the past few years, Alfie Rose's image had been carefully crafted by social media posts, television appearances, and online videos showing 'who he really was,' but his persona was so well managed by social media experts that looking into his online activity didn't provide much information.

And I wasn't interested in the successful Alfie Rose.

I was interested in the Alfie Rose that was picked on, beat up, and belittled at school.

As I walked around the streets of Logan Square, looking for my target, I took in a lot of the smells. I passed one of the old apartment buildings, and the smell reminded me of Uncle Dennis, who used to live in the area. As I got older, I came to realize that Uncle Dennis was a very bizarre man, but to a child, he was always amusing. He handed me my first dirty magazine at ten years old, passed me my first shot of whiskey at twelve, and gave me my first driving lesson on the same day. He didn't care about the law. He didn't care about any rules. That's probably why he died in prison after he was arrested for DUI for the fifth time.

After twenty minutes of walking around Logan Square, I see an old friend. And by 'old friend', I mean a person with whom I want nothing to do with, who is a drug-dealing snitch, and who will tell me anything I need to know for the right price.

"Harry."

"Shit."

That's the usual reaction I get when I say hello to scum. My reputation precedes me.

The last time I saw Homeboy Harry, I put him in the hospital. He had given me information about an investigation I was doing, and I paid him well for his time. It was a mutually profitable deal.

But then as a teenage girl walked past us, no older than fourteen, he slapped her on the bottom and told her that he had money for her.

I broke Harry's nose. I didn't appreciate his actions.

"Harry, we're going to have a chat."

"Yeah, you're lucky I can talk after last time," he snapped back.

"You'll be lucky to still be talking next time if you keep up with that attitude."

I felt like I was talking to a child. In some ways, I was.

Homeboy Harry just managed to finish high school five years ago and had been making his living on the streets ever since. With an impressive ability to remember even the smallest details, his name was well-known on the streets, in the police department, and with every PI in town.

For the right price, Harry was anyone's.

But his criminal activity wasn't why I was looking for him—he had attended the same school as Alfie Rose, and I wanted the inside scoop. When Casey dug up Alfie's yearbook, I glanced through the photos, and immediately saw Harry's cheesy grin. He looked happier in that photo, calmer, and he had a lot more weight on his bones.

The white powder that he took daily sure was an effective substance for weight loss.

"Let's talk over here," he looked up and down the street before turning down a tight alleyway.

Harry Lance cast a shadow over most people he met. His pants were a size too short, his beard was patchy, and his hair dangled over his wide shoulders. But Harry Lance looked more like a rake than a telegraph pole. He didn't look like he'd eaten an ounce of protein in years. I guess that happens when your diet is mostly drugs.

Harry stopped halfway down the alley, under an old fire escape, and leaned against the wall. A few feet from us were a collection of trash cans, a puddle of water, and I'm sure I saw a rat the size of a small dog.

"Could do with some air freshener around here, Harry."

"Can't smell much these days," he commented, sniffing like he had just done another line of crack. "But I've got a joke for you, Jack. I've been waiting to tell you this one for a while."

"Go on," I humored him. "What's the joke?"

"My friend says he's a private investigator, but I went to his office, and the sign on his door said 'Gynecologist.'" He roared with laughter. "Get it, Jack? Private?"

"I get it."

"Private." He shook his head and continued to laugh to himself. "Alright, alright. My girlfriend tried to cut off my pecker the other day. Luckily, she missed, and the cops charged her with a mis-d-wiener! Ha! Misdemeanor, mis-d-wiener! Get it, Jack? Get it?"

"For you, it would've been a small crime," I said. "And if she did cut it off, then the evidence wouldn't stand up in court."

He practically wet himself after that. It took me another five minutes to get him to stop laughing. This guy was clearly high from his own supply.

When he finally calmed down, I turned his attention to the reason I was there.

"Harry, I need you to tell me everything you know about Alfie Rose."

It took him a while to compose himself, and finally, he sighed, "You don't want to hear some more jokes? I've got a whole lot of them."

"Alfie Rose. What do you know?" I responded firmly.

"What's it worth to you, Jack? My time is valuable, you know. I'm a busy man. I have a business to run, people to see."

I took out a ten-dollar-bill from my pocket. His eyes lit up at the sight of money. This man just loved money. He was addicted to gathering it, just as much as he was addicted to wasting it on drugs.

"Double it, and I'll tell you everything I know."

Criminals are so easy. With educated people, you have to trick the information out of them. You have to outsmart them. But with men like Harry, men with a love of money and no other skills to obtain it, you only have to put the right price in front of them.

I took out another ten.

"I went to school with Alfie. He got into trouble a lot, so we were close in those early years. I was a year older than him, but we were friends, I guess because I got into trouble a lot. We sort of spurred each other on, but Alfie was smart. Really smart. He just wasn't book smart like the teachers wanted him to be. He couldn't read, you see. Dyslexic. So, he failed most classes." Harry raised a finger. "But I guess the question you want to know is—could he have done it? Could he have killed the newscaster?"

"That's what I want to know, Harry."

"Yeah, he could of. Absolutely. When he was young, he had a mean streak, our Alfie. He could snap," he clicked his fingers, "in a heartbeat. A lot of it was frustration at the teachers. He knew the answers to their questions; he just couldn't get the information out."

"Did he fight much?"

"He tried, but he always lost. He was a late bloomer, and he didn't really start growing taller until he was fifteen, maybe sixteen, and he was a skinny kid. He got picked on a lot. Beaten up. Had his lunch stolen. That sort of thing. Easy target. I guess that after he grew into the man that he is now, he wanted revenge. He wanted to get revenge against the bullies. That newscaster sure was bullying him. Maybe it was all too much."

"You're saying it wasn't so much about Gates, but all those years of torment?"

"That's what I'm saying."

"Anything else?"

"Yeah, tell the guy that I could do with some money. Give him my number. I haven't heard from him in years."

"No chance, Harry." I turned and left him to his own entertainment, walking back to the main road to catch the train. "But I'm sure we'll talk again soon."

I was due to meet Alfie in a few hours, and I had to mull over my approach. If he did it, did I feel comfortable getting him off the charges?

Maybe, because the kid wasn't paying me to have morals, but as much as I tried, as much money as Alfie offered, morals always had a way of guiding my actions.

Must've been all those Sundays that Grandma dragged me to church as a kid. Something they said must've sunk into my big old brain.

I liked Alfie, there was something about him that was magnificent, but that didn't mean a killer should be set free.

Homeboy Harry had provided good information.

But it only confused the situation more.

CHAPTER 7

A WOMAN'S scream broke the silence of the packed "L" train, creating chaos among the passengers onboard.

"They're going to kill him!" exclaimed a man in a pinstripe suit, staring wide-eyed out of a rain-streaked window at something down below at street level.

The train was stationary, waiting to enter the station, and from my position it was impossible to see what was going on.

"Oh, please no!" cried an elderly woman, glancing out of the window for the first time, recoiling a moment later in revulsion.

Others began to stare. And panic surged onboard like an electric charge.

I pushed through the crowd, but the crowded conditions slowed my progress, with people packed in tight around the window. Only when the train finally rounded the corner and we crept towards the platform did I get my first glimpse.

Down below someone was taking one hell of a beating.

An enraged mob of six or seven men were laying

into a helpless man in a brown hoodie sweatshirt, who stood, hunched over in the pouring rain, desperately clinging to a lamppost like a drowning man to a lifeline, in a vain attempt at avoiding the unforgiving sidewalk below. The blows were relentless, landing hard on his face and the back of his head, rocking it from side to side like something out of a cartoon; but somehow, he still clung to that pole. Finally, one of his attackers pried first one, then the other hand free, and dragged him by his hoodie down onto the concrete, yanking it up over his head, exposing his stark white torso underneath.

They started in on him with their boots, the flesh around his ribcage reverberating in sickening ripples as kick after kick dug deep into his bare rain-soaked gut and chest.

A soccer kick to the head, followed by a stomp, and the victim slumped into a puddle like a limp piece of meat.

The attack was fifty maybe sixty feet away, but I'd say that one of the kicks broke his jaw.

Suddenly, the train doors sprang open.

I leapt out, sprinting along the platform with critical urgency, barging past people as I went. There was no time for apologies. I powered on, my heart pounding in my chest, as I shoved my way down the cold metal steps to the sidewalk below.

There, face down in the rain, was the lifeless body of the victim, his blood mingling with the rain and seeping into a miniature waterfall off the curb into the gutter, where it sloshed about among old candy wrappers and a couple of lipstick-stained cigarette butts.

His attackers had gone. My priority was first aid.

I grabbed him by the shoulders and heaved, the dead weight of his unconscious body heavy in my arms as I rolled him onto his back.

A hideous bloodied pulp was where his face had once been. He was cut above and below both eyes which were grotesquely swollen shut and resembled a couple of juicy dark-purple plums, his lips were huge and split top and bottom, but the deepest laceration was on his forehead, which had leaked a sticky mask of blood all over his face.

As the rain poured down, the worst of the blood began to wash away.

And that's when the cold realization hit me.

I recognized what was left of that face—it was Alfie Rose.

The rain continued to fall with a brutal intensity, soaking me throughout as I knelt on the sidewalk, pumping hard on Alfie's sternum, compressing his chest up and down while his mouth emitted little wheezes, as stale air escaped from his lungs.

I searched for a pulse.

Nothing.

The rain intensified; liquid bullets exploded around me, mocking my futile attempts at resuscitation.

From out of nowhere the high-pitched wail of a siren cut through the torrent.

An orange and white van with its flashers going came skidding to a halt, swerving sideways and throwing a vile wave of dirty water in its wake.

I continued compressing Alfie's chest, while two paramedics, a male and female team, jumped from the van.

With practiced efficiency the woman thrust two fingers onto Alfie's carotid artery.

"No pulse."

Using her thumb and forefingers, she pried his painfully swollen eyelids apart, revealing one massively dilated pupil.

"Left pupil blown."

"Request back up," stated the male paramedic into his radio. "Cardiac arrest."

"Monitor," said the woman, matter-of-factly, yanking Alfie's hoodie up above his chest.

With two hands and an almighty heave, she unceremoniously ripped Alfie's expensive shirt underneath, sending mother-of-pearl buttons into the gutter.

Her colleague grabbed the defibrillator.

One electrode pad above Alfie's right pec, the other below his left pec, and they checked the screen.

"He's in VF."

"Keep compressing, Sir," she instructed me, hitting the charge button on the machine, while I continued pumping Alfie's chest. "Charging to 200 Jules!"

Beep, beep, beep, beeeeeeeeeeeeeeeeep.

"Hands off!" she ordered, then pressed a big orange button with an icon of a lightning bolt, delivering a two and a half thousand-volt punch to Alfie's limp carcass.

He spasmed on the ground.

Nothing.

She took over the chest compressions.

"You've done a great job. If he's got any chance, it's because of you."

I imagined she said that to everyone, whether it was true or not.

Her colleague placed more equipment on the sidewalk and knelt in front of Alfie's head.

"No sign of breath. We'd better get some oxygen into him—I'll start bagging."

Placing a face mask connected to an inflatable silicone bag over Alfie's nose and mouth, he began pumping oxygen into Alfie's lungs.

His chest started to rise and fall then suddenly stopped.

There was a gurgling sound.

"I'm having trouble here. He's regurgitating vomit. He needs suction!"

Quickly whipping the mask off his face, he stuffed a plastic pipe into Alfie's swollen and bloodied mouth.

A sound akin to a high-powered vacuum cleaner hummed, as blood, filth and vomit was sucked from Alfie's clogged airway.

Once more he placed the mask on Alfie and

pumped hard on the silicone bag, working it like a bellows.

"He's got a terrible airway!" he yelled, whipping off the mask again and grabbing another piece of thin flexible 6-inch pipe, which he rammed into Alfie's nostril.

'Bagging' commenced again, and Alfie's lungs started to inflate.

"We've got an airway, but it's still not great."

"Give him some adrenaline."

"How much?"

"The max!"

Time spun by in a whirl: another tube here, an injection there, more oxygen and a second shock from the defibrillator, but still no response.

Back up arrived: a second van with two male EMTs.

Beep, beep, beep, beeeeeeeeeeeeeeeeeep.

"Hands off!" ordered the female paramedic, as Alfie received his third two-and-a-half-thousand-volt payload to the chest.

Suddenly the defibrillator's screen beeped to life with the spikes and dips of a heart's electrical activity.

"We've got a pulse! VF to sinus rhythm."

"He's taking breaths."

"Get him into the van."

With a rigid spine board, the four responders heaved Alfie into the ambulance.

"Check blood pressure," said the female paramedic, wrapping a cuff around Alfie's upper arm as one of the backup team jumped into the driver's seat.

I jumped onboard too. The doors slammed. The sirens screamed. And we were off.

A motorized pneumatic sound struck up as the cuff inflated.

"85 over 48. He's low. Give him some fluid, 500cc, and 50 micrograms of adrenaline."

As we hurtled our way to the hospital, the paramedics fought frantically to save Alfie, pumping him full of liquids, drugs and oxygen in a desperate attempt to preserve his teetering life.

Suddenly, he began gagging violently.

There were signs of life, he was waking up with a great big tube down the back of his throat, inserted for clear access to his lungs so the oxygen bag could take full effect.

In an instant, "bagging" stopped and the tube was whipped from his throat.

Alfie lay distraught and confused, wailing in pain like a wounded beast.

"Give him five milligrams of morphine."

If it looked like good news, it was fleeting.

Lying supine, he began vomiting forcefully. His mouth filled and he started to choke.

"We've lost control of his airway!"

The monitor's alarm rang out.

"We're losing him!"

More frantic suctioning and bagging.

"O2 stats are dropping… down to 85.'

"Blood pressure dropping. 70 over 40. Heart rate 122."

"O2 stats down to 82!'

Tubes, injections, more fluid, adrenaline and some anti-nausea medication followed in a bewildering, high-speed succession.

I looked on helplessly as they worked.

One of the EMTs grabbed his radio.

"This is EMT Richard Logan. We're ten minutes away with a priority 1 post-cardiac arrest patient. He's been badly assaulted; head, face and chest are in a terrible state. Looks like a blow to the chest might have put him in VF arrest. He was in VF arrest when we got to him but got ROSC after three shocks. He's now hypotensive at 70 over 40 and we're having trouble keeping his airway clear. Currently O2 stats are 88 percent and we're giving him some assisted ventilations through an iGel. We checked his pupils and the left one is dilated, so it looks like he's got a bad head injury as well…"

A lot of this I didn't understand but his last words were clear enough.

"…Not sure if he's going to make it to the ER."

CHAPTER 8

LAURA CALLED again.

This time she was checking on me. When she asked, 'Are you okay, Jack?' I almost fell off my chair. It wasn't often that Laura had shown any sort of care towards me—mostly she spent her time saying that I, a tattooed brute, wasn't good enough for her very smart, very witty, and very beautiful, princess.

Most of the time, I think she was right—Claire was way out of my league. She was too nice, too kind, and too loving for a lump of hardened muscle like me.

Laura had seen me on the news trying to save Alfie's life.

Of course, while I was trying to revive the kid, there were numerous people standing around with their phones recording the moment. For the life of me, I couldn't figure out why they would've wanted to record it. Videos used to be about recording a moment that you wanted to remember, a moment that you wanted to live on past the worn memories.

Who in their right mind would want to remember the moment that a kid almost died on the sidewalk?

In the end, I figured the answer was fame. One kid that videoed my actions said that the news networks could use his videos, and he boasted that he received an extra thousand followers on social media after that. Good for you, kid—you've got people who've you never met following you because you took a video of someone almost dying. What a hero.

Laura's concern for me didn't last long.

Once she knew I was fine, the conversation turned back to Claire, and more specifically, the person that gave Claire's killer the gun. I lied and told her that I may have a fresh lead, but I'm sure she didn't believe me.

The case had kept me awake for years, driving me almost insane with insomnia. I had already looked down every avenue, searched through every clue, gone through the case a thousand times. I hadn't missed anything; I was sure of that.

But Laura was a dying woman who wanted justice for her deceased daughter—I understood her need for closure. I accepted long ago that I would never have closure, that the nightmares would continue to haunt me until the day I died.

If my time was coming to a close, would I feel the same as Laura? Most likely.

Inevitably, I blamed myself for everything. It seemed to be the only way to avoid the torment of knowing that someone out there may have been responsible for Claire's death, and hadn't paid the price for it.

I also blamed myself for what happened to Alfie Rose on the sidewalk.

I'd arranged to meet Alfie and had reluctantly agreed to his request for it to be at his favorite watering hole: British themed pub, The Sir Robert Benjamin, opposite Armitage 'L' station in Lincoln Park.

I'd tried to talk him out of it, for us to meet at his penthouse, but he was adamant. He said he was going stir-crazy inside, that he needed fresh air, needed to taste some freedom in case it was his last; and, that he was going for a drink whether I met him or not.

Maybe it had been a bluff. Maybe I should have refused him point blank.

But he was a big guy and I wasn't his babysitter. However, if he died, I knew I'd be carrying an extra load of guilt to add to the one already hanging heavy around my neck from Claire's death.

It was touch and go, but after a hard-fought battle Alfie made it to the hospital, just.

Four major surgeries passed, and he was taken off the critical list. A painful week dripped by.

Then, at the start of week two, he finally woke up.

My relief was palpable.

The media had a field day. Alfie's story was running on the front page of every major newspaper, leading every major television bulletin, and was trending on social media. His supporters became even louder, and his opponents even louder still.

The debate quickly became less about Alfie, less

about Brian Gates, and more about left versus right. By the time Alfie woke up, his story was lost in a verbal assault of barbs, insults, and lightly veiled threats between opposing groups.

How it even came to this, I still don't understand. How could someone believe their own ideas so much that they're willing to get into a confrontation with strangers over them?

Long ago, I accepted that some people had different ideas than me. However, if they disagreed too aggressively, they met my fist.

To me, that seemed fair.

The investigation was met with numerous dead ends—no extra video surveillance footage around the dressing room that Gates used, no additional social media posts, and no further witnesses came forward. I had been trying to keep a low profile, out of the way of Alfie's defense team, but that was becoming harder to do as the case grew and grew.

My contacts on the street knew nothing, my police contacts wouldn't talk about the case, and my contacts in the television industry all thought Alfie did it. Casey worked hard on any missing internet links, anything that could be tied to that night, but she also came to nothing.

We weren't the only ones working for him—the defense team that Alfie hired seemed solid, if unspectacular.

They fronted the media as Alfie's spokespersons, answering any and all questions. It seemed to me like they were enjoying the spotlight a little too much, but every interview was free advertising for their law firm, I suppose.

In every interview they conducted, they were clearly positioning themselves for Alfie to roll over on a deal.

Which had me thinking—did he hire me because he was guilty?

I had no answer to that question. How could I? An innocent person who didn't want to go to prison and a guilty person who didn't want to go to prison would most likely be acting the same way in this situation. The only conclusion that I could come to was that he hired me because he hated the thought of spending time behind bars.

The more I saw of the kid, the more videos I viewed online, the more I liked him. He was fresh, energetic, and had an attractive energy around him. His positivity practically jumped right out of the screen.

If he was innocent, it would break my heart to see him go behind bars.

He didn't deserve that; no innocent person did.

It was unlike me to get emotionally involved in a case but somehow this one was different.

When I finally got to see him in the hospital, he could barely speak, the brace holding his shattered jaw together made sure of that. He had two fractures in his jaw, some missing teeth, and three broken ribs. His nose looked slightly off center, there was bruising down his neck and arms, and both his eyes were still black. He had the best care that money could buy, the best room in the ward, but even that didn't seem to ease the anguish in his eyes.

Pain is pain, no matter how expensive your doctors are.

He said a few words, and I told him quietly that the case was progressing. I wanted to sell him false hope, give him something positive to look forward to, but it seemed irresponsible, no matter how much it would lighten his mood in that moment.

He looked to me as a symbol of hope anyway, a last chance to get out of this mess.

As I stared at him, all stitches, tubes, drips and monitors, something took me by surprise: the horror of what happened to Claire came flooding back. I didn't last long in the hospital after that. I ran outside, searched for the closest bar, and tried to drown those thoughts away.

Those thoughts had been suppressed for many years, and I didn't want to confront them. Not then, not ever.

Over the next few days, every time I thought about Alfie in the hospital, images flashed before me of what I knew must have transpired in that classroom. I tried not to think of her, to concentrate on work, but it was useless. She was there more often than I could ever admit.

I tried to conjure up the good times, the precious bliss we'd shared together so as to banish the darkness, but try as I might, it was always the horror that rose to the surface.

To be haunted by the person you love is a tragedy.

I hated those thoughts.

And I hated myself for thinking them.

All that remained was her memory and even that I had tainted.

I suppressed her as best I could and tried to focus on the investigation; on Alfie.

And that's when I realized, the two were becoming meshed in my mind, inextricably linked. I was no longer just fighting for Alfie; whether I liked it or not, I was now also fighting for the memory of Claire.

And if I fought for Claire, then all hell would come with me.

CHAPTER 9

SOMETIMES THE smallest clue can reveal a giant hidden truth: something out of sync, unusual, unlikely, improbable, or maybe just plain curious; something tiny that raises a simple question that becomes the beginning of a thread, which, if followed, leads to a revelation at its end, palatable or otherwise.

It began with a tiny detail of a photograph taken on a long weekend in the fall.

Claire and I had been staying with her brother, Ben, his wife Nicky, and their four-year-old daughter Alana, at a vacation cabin in the Manistee National Forest on the eastern shores of Lake Michigan. I enjoyed going up there, it had good fishing, camping, and hunting. It was a nice place to unwind in the great outdoors and enjoy what life is all about. They'd rented the place as a celebration; Ben had just scored a long sought after promotion in the Chicago Police Department and Nicky announced her second pregnancy.

A great time was had by all and after we got home, Ben and Nicky sent us a couple of photographs of the trip as mementos. Onto the fridge went a photo of us sharing a meal together on the final evening and, as typically happens, soon after it was forgotten about.

It was only when it slipped from under the fridge magnet and drifted down onto the floor a month later that I looked at it, or, more accurately, saw it, for the first time. Sure, I would have glanced at it in a cursory, oh, that's nice, kind of way, but as I picked it up from the kitchen tiles something registered that I had previously missed.

It was all in the eyes.

There in Alana's right eye was a tiny glowing dot of gold.

Taken by itself it might have been an anomaly, a quirk of the flash or light, so I dug around for some other photos of her. And there it was again. And again. Always in her right eye. Although invisible in person, there it was in all the photos.

"You need to get Alana's eye checked out," I told Nicky on the phone, explaining that the strange golden glow could be an indication of a tumor.

She was shocked and worried and took Alana straight to the pediatrician. He couldn't detect anything but recommended she immediately take her to a specialist for a second opinion. It was then they discovered that Alana was practically blind in her right eye; that the reflective golden dot was the result of a mass of white in her eye caused by Coats' Disease, a condition that, if left untreated, could necessitate the entire eye's removal.

Alana was lucky, it was caught early and after four operations she was given the all clear. Ben and Nicky made such a big song and dance about me having saved their little girl's eye, that they were eternally in my debt and that I was to let them know if ever there was anything they could do for me.

To be honest, it was all a bit embarrassing.

I had done nothing that anyone else wouldn't do under the circumstances, and I never thought I'd be asking for that favor. But with Alfie in such a precarious position, and time ticking, I decided to hit Ben up for assistance. Not only was he a Chicago cop but, as luck would have it, had worked closely for several years with Alfie's arresting officer. I needed some inside info; specifically, who else apart from Alfie had been considered for Brian Gates' murder? It was a tricky ask, but desperate times called for desperate measures, and Alfie's predicament was about as desperate as they got and getting worse by the day.

I'd not seen or spoken to Ben or Nicky since Claire's funeral. They'd written to me several times and tried calling but I'd shut them out.

It wasn't personal.

I needed to be alone, to deal with the pain in my way, on my terms, not anybody else's. The letters had long since ceased and they probably resented my lack of contact. Seeing people who knew and loved Claire was likely to rip off the mental and emotional scar, opening up the wound again. I'd built up my mental armor in the years since Claire's murder, and, in truth, I dreaded taking it off.

But I was committed now.

As I drove towards their place, on the fringes of Wolf Lake, about 45 minutes from the city, I mulled over what I was going to say, while my ever enthusiastic golden retriever, Winston, barked and panted away in the passenger seat next to me, his eyes darting left and right, randomly jumping from one source of interest to another.

The two of us had become inseparable since Claire's murder, me and this comically silly dog. Claire had got him from a shelter for abused animals.

I'd initially been against the idea of getting a dog, we didn't have the space, he would be an unwanted commitment, and anyway I wasn't a dog person.

Or so I thought.

It hardly seemed that way now. Winston had pretty much won me over the day he trotted in through our door, and I loved him to pieces. Our favorite thing was to hit the trails together, heading up and over hills, through forests, along the shore, anywhere outside the city. We did it whenever we got the chance, which had been less and less of late thanks to a deluge of work, but when we did it was bliss. We'd work each other out hard and by the end we'd both be spent, but it always felt like I'd unloaded a pile of mental baggage on the trail.

Ben was on his day off, spending it fishing on the lake. I'd called ahead of time and spoken to Nicky. It was an awkward call, but she told me where to find him.

She sounded reluctant and mentioned Ben had recently lost his partner in the line of duty: he was shot in the head in a gangbanger shootout in Chicago's Englewood neighborhood. Nicky said he'd taken it hard and was spending more and more time alone.

I found him staring at the tip of his rod as if in a trance, watching it bob up and down on the surface of the water, practically oblivious to everything else, as if the world beyond that rod tip ceased to exist.

It was windy today, but too much so to be a benefit; a bit of chop on the water's surface is a fisherman's friend, it reduces visibility underwater, so flaws in your bait are concealed, to an extent, from the fish; and waves along the shore stir up the bottom so the bigger fish get out and about to feed on those lower down the food chain.

Today it was practically blowing a gale.

Ben would be lucky to catch anything, but I knew that it wasn't really fish he was after but head space and solitude, however fleeting.

"Ben!" I exclaimed, doing my best to sound upbeat. "Are they biting?"

"Jack," he said, half smiling half letting out a sigh. "Nicky mentioned you'd be coming down."

"How are things?"

"Things are good. You?"

"Good."

We were both lying—and least about the things that really mattered—and what's more, we both knew as much. But neither of us were wear your heart on your sleeve kind of guys, so we carried on the charade, it was standard operating procedure for the likes of us to put up a stoic front. And I make no apology for it.

"Sorry if I seem a bit down," said Ben. "Some guy stole my anti-depressants yesterday. I'm upset, but I hope he's happy."

We both laughed as the joke demanded, but it was clearly forced.

"Did you hear about the new restaurant on the moon?" It was traditional that we traded bad jokes, so I came prepared with my worst. "Great food. No atmosphere."

He laughed, genuinely, more than the joke deserved.

"What do you call an Italian guy with a rubber toe?" He started laughing again. "Roberto."

I tried not to laugh, but I couldn't help it. It was a release of nervous pressure, a way to let the tension out.

So commenced a protracted round of small talk, centered around fishing: the tides and the wind conditions, his new rod, the type of bait he was using. I knew he didn't want to discuss what had happened to his partner and he knew I didn't want to discuss Claire, so why even bother? We both respected that and carried on in this way, with occasional breaks to play fight with Winston, for about 15 minutes, when Ben finally broke the deadlock.

"But you didn't come down here to talk to me about fishing, did you Jack?"

"No. I did not."

"So why are you here, why now?"

"I need to ask a favor."

He raised his eyebrows and looked at me in a way that begged the question: and that favor is?

"I've taken on a case, one that you'll be familiar with, and one that I don't have the luxury of time to solve—the murder of Brian Gates."

"You're working for Alfie Rose?" He shook his head incredulously. "And you think he's innocent, do you? Come on, get real, Jack! All the evidence points to this guy. He lost control, got angry after Gates bullied him, and he snapped. Hit him a few times. In my line of work, you see it all the time. You can't really think he's innocent. No way."

"As a matter of fact, I do." I replied.

I was stretching the truth.

I was open minded as to what really happened that night. Sure, I thought Alfie was probably innocent, but at the same time I hadn't ruled out the possibility that he'd done it or had a hand in it, only this seemed much less likely to me. There was nuance to my position, as an investigator there had to be, but nuance wasn't going to get results with Ben. If he thought I was convinced of Alfie's innocence, then he'd be far more likely to help, so I made my opinion sound cast iron.

"There's nothing I can give you," he said. "I wasn't involved in the case. And even if I was, you know I can't divulge information about ongoing police work. You know how it works. I can't go sniffing around because my, well, I suppose ex-brother-in-law…"

He paused for a moment, and so did I.

Ex-brother-in-law?

I hadn't really thought about it, but I suppose he was right. There was nothing tying us together anymore. I hadn't seen them in years, I hadn't even talked to them, and we had no blood relations.

"Sorry, Jack. That's not how I meant it." He turned back to his rod tip with a pained expression.

"The kid's innocent, Ben." I wasn't going to push the notion of family any further, I'd had enough of that sort of talk recently. "Justice isn't served by the wrong guy going down for murder, less so if he's killed inside, which you know is a real probability. He'll be dead within a year."

He looked unmoved, but I continued regardless.

"Do you remember telling me once that it was the pursuit of justice that first led you to join the force? Things might have gotten blurred over the years but that's what I'm after too, only we're approaching it from different angles. If you're right and Alfie Rose is guilty then no amount of chicanery from me will help him. But I want the full picture. I want to know who else was a suspect, and why?"

"It wasn't my case, Jack."

"I know; it was Detective O'Reilly's. It's hardly a secret that you guys are close, real close—best man at your wedding; I was there too, remember? Look, I know how it is, you would have discussed it, probably over a couple of beers, right?"

"I'm not in a position to say."

"I need this favor, Ben. And as much as it pains me to say it, you owe me one."

With a reluctant sigh, he turned from his rod tip and looked me in the eye.

He knew I was right.

"Firstly, for the record, I think you're wrong. I think you're barking up the wrong tree and that the gamer did it. Guilty as charged and he'll be found so, you'll see. But if you insist on pursuing this fantasy, then I concede, I do owe you. How could I not?"

He looked about furtively.

We were alone, the wind was howling and there was no chance of us being heard by someone right next to us, let alone the only other person in sight, a dog walker over a hundred feet away, but he glanced about regardless, just to make sure.

"Off the record, of course."

I nodded.

"Two names: Kelly Holmes and Pat Packman. Both were suspects, but that doesn't mean much. These sorts of cases generate lots of suspects early on, it's where the evidence points that matters and it pointed to Rose."

"Why them?"

"Holmes for obvious reasons: ex-wife, open about her hatred of Gates, and happy to express it at any given opportunity, but I imagine that won't come as news to you. As for Packman, well, he was more interesting, something I imagine will come as news to you is that Brian Gates had been putting the feelers out for a new producer. Seems like he was ready to drop Packman, to cut him loose after all those years together and either find a replacement or go solo, with Gates also taking an executive producer credit. Gates was ready to take his show to a new network and was in the final stages of negotiation, only Packman wouldn't be joining him."

"Did Packman know about this?"

"Hard to say. If he did, it's motive. But so what? All the physical evidence pointed to your boy. And still does."

"Anything else you can give me?"

"Not really, only that Gates was having multiple affairs at the time of his death."

"Any names?"

"Only one I remember was Lizzie Guthrie."

"At the time of his death?"

"Yeah."

"You're sure about that? I mean, I know Lizzie Guthrie had a fling with him a long time ago, but you're saying it happened recently too?"

"Look, I'm just telling you what I heard. I don't know if it was serious or a casual thing, but word is, it was more than a one off. Any more than that, I couldn't say."

This was interesting, got me thinking, and something was falling into place.

I thanked Ben for his counsel, passed on my best wishes to his family, then made my excuses and left.

I had something to work with now; Alfie had a chance. Not much of one but a chance, nonetheless. I might have been the only person in his corner, but I never bet against myself, not once I got started on a hunch.

Things were really starting to get interesting, but this was no simple matter of curiosity, it was a murder inquiry. And murder, after all, is not a board game. Murder is not about motive or alibi; it is about death, and all the hideousness that comes with it.

And if truth be told, I had a foreboding feeling there was more around the corner.

CHAPTER 10

THE POLICE did their best to control the mayhem, holding back the opposing crowds who were barricaded in on either side of the street. Bottles, placards, even shoes, flew from one side to the other, as if to punctuate the deafening verbal abuse, but every so often a fanatic would break free and launch an attack in person, arms flailing, and face enraged with destructive intent. That's when the batons came out, and the offender got dragged away by Chicago's finest, kicking and screaming, to a nearby van to hear their rights.

I had seen them on the way into the hospital, the Brian Gates obsessives and the Alfie Rose devotees, each hurling insults at the other while jabbing their signs into the air: labelling Alfie a murderer and castigating him to hell and beyond, or proclaiming his innocence and wishing him a speedy recovery.

Take your pick.

There was hardly any middle ground in their positions but somehow the proponents all seemed the same to me. That people would get so emotional about individuals they had never met, and never would, because they had seen them on the television or Instagram, was a surreal spectacle to watch. Of the many things I struggled to fathom in this world, the cult of celebrity was one of the biggest.

It was hard to leave Alfie in the hospital, no matter how good the care was that he was getting. But I was no use to him in there. He needed me on the outside doing what I did best: solving a puzzle and quickly. The pressure was on, but I liked it that way.

Urgency always brought out the best in me.

I'd increased the workload for Casey and me to get the job done, no matter what. There just wasn't the time to play by the rules anymore. If corners had to be cut and rules needed to be bent or broken, then so be it. I wasn't above it, and it wouldn't be the first time either.

As I strode along the hospital corridor towards the exit doors, I felt focused. The time was now, and I was ready for action. As the automatic doors slid open, I was hit by a deafening wall of noise.

The crowds were in a frenzy and had morphed into something different. A new contingent had joined the fray: a hodgepodge of anti-fascists and militant feminists had aligned with the Alfie Rose side, and a group of Alt-Right and freedom of speech patriots had aligned themselves on 'The Gates' side.

If they'd been angry earlier, they were enraged now.

I stood motionless for a second and watched, incredulous, but also bemused, at the insanity that stretched before me.

"I'm a woman not an object!" yelled a protester, whose sign repeated the phrase, emblazoned in big red letters, which I understood in the context of Brian Gates' womanizing, but some of the other signs were just nuts, and had nothing to do with either Gates or Rose.

"There's no biological sex!" announced one.

"Gender equality is fantastic: Women deserve to be punched in the head more often!" declared another.

"Alt-right is not all right!"

"Free speech does not equal hate speech!"

The slogans went on.

Both sides had hijacked the killing and memory of one man and the due process of another for their own political agenda. Gates would have hated both groups with equal passion, but he was no longer here to care.

It was Alfie whom this nonsense was really hurting, stirring up more anger against him and diminishing further any hope of a fair trial. He'd never waded into identity politics before, but somehow his name was being traduced and associated with the social justice warriors who hated Brian Gates, simply because of his impending trial.

Suddenly a purple-haired freak-show with a pair of matching goggles on her forehead threw a bottle high into the air. If she was aiming at 'The Gates' brigade then it was a very poor effort, indeed. More time playing sports and less time on the internet would have served her well, as her pitching skills were useless, and the bottle's looping trajectory saw it inadvertently heading in my direction.

I stood still and watched it descend in the way you do when you've subconsciously calculated that something heading towards you is thankfully going to land short of the mark.

With a loud crack it impacted with the ground, exploding not ten feet from where I stood, spreading out across the asphalt in a thousand tiny crystals that showered my shoes in flecks of glass.

"Yeah!" "Woohoo!" screamed her comrades like demented morons.

"U-S-A! U-S-A!" chanted a group of what looked like bikers in retaliation, waving the stars and stripes in the air.

Things were heating up, alright.

And another new element wasn't helping.

Several film crews had arrived on the scene and were capturing the action for the evening news, inadvertently stirring the crowds into a maelstrom of anger, with each vying for the top spot on the news. A couple of them were talking on camera but one appeared to be taking an altogether more hands on approach: Hugh Guthrie, giving a Brian Gatester what looked like a prearranged signal: a none-too-subtle double nod of the head accompanied with an expression that silently screamed, Now!

Suddenly the man leapt over the cordon and ran

toward the other side screaming. He didn't get far. Two steps in and the inevitable happened when several burly officers crashed on top of him and smashed him hard into the ground.

Luckily, the concrete broke his fall.

Hugh's crew caught it all on camera.

Typical Hugh; his image might have been a principled Mr. Wholesome, but I knew from when he'd paid me to dig up dirt on a rival that the reality was somewhat different. If they appear squeaky clean, then the chances are they're the exact opposite.

As attacks on the other side went it was utterly ineffective, but it sure would have made great footage. The satisfied grin plastered across Hugh and his cameraman's face left me in little doubt that this was the point.

Hugh turned and caught sight of me.

It was clear I'd caught him in the act.

He held up his hands and twiddled them with a mock smile, as if to say, "You got me, Valentine."

I walked over and shook my head.

"Inciting a riot for the benefit of your own ratings? Isn't that fake news, Hugh? You know, our president doesn't like that sort of thing. Always going on about it, and aren't you a big supporter of his? Conservative, trustworthy newsman that you are. Don't tell me it's all a deceptive façade, Hugh."

"Oh, come on, Jack. I didn't do it; I just encouraged it to happen. That's what news is these days. That's how the business works. This isn't the seventies, Jack, we're in a new era now. You've got to make your own news. And don't tell me that you're that naïve, Jack. We're a business, like any other business, and you've gotta to give the public what they want."

"What, idiots hijacking the near killing of my client to make their own spurious unconnected political statement?"

Hugh could see I wasn't in the mood for his shenanigans.

"So how is the kid, you get to visit him?"

"Is that concern for Alfie's wellbeing, or are you trying to get the inside scoop? I tell you anything and boom!... Sources close to Alfie Rose inform us that his current condition…come on Hugh, you know I'm not going to fall for that. Give me some credit, you know me better than that."

"You can't blame a guy for trying. The upcoming murder trial is big news. In fact, it's the hottest topic in town, by far. And everyone's got an opinion, our latest poll has Alfie guilty by seventy to thirty, nothing scientific, of course, but a good yardstick of public sentiment."

"Idiots who call into live television polls are hardly representative of the public's sentiment."

"That's my viewers you're referring to there, whom I happen to hold in very high regard."

"Contempt, more like it—mainly because there aren't enough of them and the ones there are don't tune in regularly enough."

"Very funny, Jack. Come on, let's not get off on the wrong foot here. We go way back, you and me; helped each other in the past, didn't we? All I'm saying is, it looks like you've got your work cut out with this one, and if I was a betting man, which I most certainly am not, my money would be on him going down. Unanimous verdict too."

I glanced around at the raging crowds.

"What do you make of all this?" I asked.

"I'd be lying if I said it didn't make for some great footage, but I've never seen anything quite like it before. Gates was obviously a very polarizing figure, and by all accounts Rose is too, but all of this other stuff, all the crazies it's attracted, the extreme left and extreme right, is something else. Some people just have nothing better to do, and of course it's nothing to do with the case, but it is great theater, really great theater. And that's what news is all about when it comes down to it, Jack."

"No tolerance for intolerance!" yelled a skinny 'soyboy' at close quarters, nearly making Hugh and me go deaf in the process.

Hugh looked from him to me and rolled his eyes with a smile.

"I don't need to tell you that time's ticking, Jack. You got any leads you're working on?"

"I'm following a few, you know how it is. Tell me, how well do you know Pat Packman?"

"Packman, you think he's your man?"

"I didn't say that, but he's a person of interest,

alright. You hear anything about Gates planning to drop Packman as producer?"

"You're kidding? Where did you hear that?"

"Can't say, but it's credible."

"Wow, I knew they didn't always see eye to eye, but professionally their partnership was a success, I thought it was as solid as a rock. There would have been a lot of money riding on that partnership, if Gates was calling an end to it, then… wow, that's big."

"I know."

"Thinking about it though, it makes sense."

"How so?"

"I saw them having a, how can I put it, forthright exchange, at the charity auction. In the bathroom of all places. I didn't catch much, just the tail end of things, but something I did catch was Packman telling Gates that no one was going to put him out to pasture."

"Have you mentioned this to anyone before?"

"Didn't seem relevant to be honest, those two were always at it. It would have been noteworthy if they weren't fighting… not that they were."

"Did anyone else hear this?"

"Nope, I was the only other person in there, I walked in on them arguing and soon after they shut up and left. But that's how it was with them, blazing arguments one minute then a quick reset and back to business the next."

"Or perhaps not back to business this time."

"But why now?" asked Hugh. "Even after Packman's wife left him for Gates, the two still ended up prioritizing their work together, so why cut him loose now?"

"Well, that's the question, isn't it?"

I paused for a moment before proceeding with my next line of questioning, which seemed likely to be a difficult one.

"Look, Hugh, there's something I want to ask you."

"Oh, yeah, this sounds ominous."

"Yeah, and it's something you won't want to hear."

"This is a first, the great Jack Valentine tip-toeing around a subject. Well go on, spit it out, let's hear it."

"Fair enough. It concerns Lizzie."

Hugh's eyes widened.

"The thing is, I have information to suggest that Lizzie and Brian Gates' relationship was not so much a one-off thing of the distant past but might also have included the recent present."

"Back the hell up there, Valentine! Don't you dare drag my family into your sordid investigation," he yelled, jabbing a finger in my direction. "I've never heard such an unfounded claptrap in all my life. This conversation is finished!"

And that was it, Hugh turned on his heel and stormed off.

Was it the reaction of a man who had just heard for the first time that his wife had cheated, or was it the reaction of a man who already knew but couldn't bear anyone bringing it up?

I wasn't sure, but one thing was certain: I would follow the evidence wherever it took me.

No matter the offense or hurt it caused.

And no matter the danger.

The truth had to come out.

CHAPTER 11

I'D WATCHED Packman over the weekend and didn't like what I'd seen.

On Sunday morning he'd had three separate arguments with strangers. The first was a road rage incident where some guy had pulled out a fraction too early in front of him, causing Packman to momentarily slow down. It was enough to cause a raised eyebrow or a little tut-tut from most of us, but Packman went berserk. Out of the window came the middle finger and an endless tirade of shouting and cussing. Not satisfied, Packman hit the gas.

Overtaking the offending automobile, he cut in front of it and jumped on the brakes, bringing both to a standstill in the heavy traffic. Leaping from his vehicle, he paced menacingly towards the other driver's door. With an almighty yank he pulled it open and got in the guy's face, jabbing a finger at him, while yelling a blue streak.

The other guy turned white and backed down.

And then, as if a 'reset' button had been hit, Packman strolled back to his vehicle, got in, and drove off calmly as if nothing had happened.

It didn't take long for things to heat up again.

Ten minutes later he pulled up at a coffee shop for a quick bagel and a strong injection of caffeine. No incidents occurred inside, in fact, Packman smiled cordially and even attempted to charm the pretty girl serving customers —albeit badly and unreceptively— but when he stepped outside the red mist descended once more.

A male parking enforcement officer was slapping a ticket on his windshield.

At first, Packman tried insincere politeness, in a futile attempt at getting the fine revoked, but when it became apparent that it wasn't going to work, he dropped the nice guy routine and let it rip.

"Don't take it out on me!"

"Take what out on you, sir?"

"That you're about fifty pound overweight and one monumental loser."

"There's no need to get personal. I'm just doing my job."

"Yeah, that's right, a loser's job," spat Packman. "Have you got kids?"

"Yeah, but I don't see what that has to do with anything."

"How does it feel when they say to you, 'Daddy, what do you do for a job?' and you have to reply, 'I'm a meter maid, kids.' Imagine their shame that their father is such a failure in life, or the embarrassment they suffer at school when someone asks them what you do. Do they admit that this is all you've amounted to, or do they lie and pretend you've got a different job, something less pathetic? Probably lie, I reckon. And who can blame them."

The man stood open-mouthed in shock, genuinely hurt and offended.

But that was Packman's intention.

Packman flipped the bird again and this time held it right in the man's face, while glaring at him with real venom and menace.

For a second, I thought it might spill over into violence, that Packman was about to punch the man, but perhaps mindful of the people watching, and the nearby video cameras, he went no further. Ripping the ticket from the windshield, he scrunched it up, got in his car and threw the ticket in the back.

The engine fired up with an ear-splitting rev, and he tore off down the street, tires squealing as he went.

The third incident was the worst according to what I heard about from Casey. We'd switched duties to minimize our chances of being spotted: she took over the tail, I headed back to the office to follow up on other lines of inquiry.

After a few hours of her following him, we met up to swap places again, this time outside a shooting range. Being Sunday, Packman had time on his hands and had headed down for a bit of recreational target practice.

"How was he?" I asked Casey, when meeting her in the car lot outside.

"In a word: nuts," she said, shaking her head. "He

got into a crazy argument with some old grandma in a wheelchair before he went inside, after he pulled up in a disabled parking spot without a permit. The old girl, who had her placard and plate on display, arrived moments earlier in the only other disabled spot next to him, and when she spotted Packman without any permit or disability, she gave it to him with both barrels—figuratively speaking, you understand, since we're at a gun range, and all."

I laughed.

"She might have looked all meek and sweet, but wow, that girl had spirit," continued Casey with a smile, ever the supporter of the underdog. "Down came her wheelchair ramp and over she rolled, practically squaring up to Packman for a fight, who by this stage was standing next to his car. She wasn't taking any nonsense and went straight for him, lecturing him on how he was preventing her from accessing essential services in the form of her second amendment rights to bear arms as part of a well-regulated militia."

"Beautiful!" I said, bummed to have missed that one.

"She kept calling him 'sonny boy' too."

"Nice touch."

"Yeah, I thought so," said Casey, "That really got him mad. The two of them went at it for five minutes straight, yelling back and forth, neither of them backing down. I think Packman got increasingly agitated that he wasn't intimidating her."

"So, what happened?"

"The manager finally came out to see what all the commotion was about. At which point Packman acts all innocent; like it's an honest mistake, and claims he's been civil and polite in the face of unwarranted abuse from her."

"What, like he's the victim?"

"You got it!"

"What a piece of work."

"Yeah, he clearly didn't want to get blacklisted from the club, so he does an about-face and moves his car, while the old girl rolls on inside, muttering abuse under her breath—only that wasn't the end of it."

"Oh yeah?"

"Yeah. Packman waits in his car for a while until the dust has settled, then goes to his trunk, rummages around and retrieves a 6-inch nail. He then slinks over to her car, gives a furtive glance around to see if anyone or any cameras are watching, then wedges the nail behind her rear right tire and the concrete, so when she reverses… Bang!"

"You're joking?"

Casey glanced towards the woman's vehicle with a "take a look for yourself" expression.

And there, sure enough, was the nail wedged up against her tire at a 45-degree angle.

"I'm kind of tempted to go inside and tell her, in the hope that she takes it upon herself to administer some on the spot justice, in the form of a bullet to

Packman's head," said Casey with a little nod of approval.

"Take it easy there, partner. Let's see if we can pin Gates' murder on the scumbag first."

"I hear you," replied Casey. "He's certainly got the temperament for it."

To be honest, that Packman had proved himself to be such a complete and utter lowlife was a surprise. Not that I ever thought he might be a nice guy, you understand, only that his level of anger was unexpected.

Still, often when following targets their true personality leaks out in front of you, a little here and a little there, but with Packman it wasn't so much leaking as flooding. He was thoroughly obnoxious and frequently angry—not the sort of person you want to see with a firearm in his hands. But it was time for me to take over and follow him inside, and I was curious to see if he was a good shot.

Before bidding Casey goodbye and heading into the shooting range, I swiped the nail from under the car's tire.

"Find a safe place for this," I said to Casey with a nod towards Packman's car.

I found Packman at the far end of the firing lanes, practicing with a Glock pistol, shooting at paper targets with pictures of zombies on them, one of several unconventional target options offered at the booth inside. To his credit, the guy was a fair shot, not exceptional, but certainly above average.

I'd signed up for a bit of practice myself, as no matter how accurate someone else is, watching them endlessly shoot and reload is hardly a stimulating way to spend your time. As I went to my firing lane, I spotted the woman in the wheelchair two lanes down, decked out in a shoulder sling to help her better brace and stabilize the beast of a semi-automatic she had cocked, locked and ready to rock, in her hands.

She let it rip with a short burst, every one hitting home in the center of the target.

Not bad, I mused.

I took aim and then fired at my own target—this time a conventional, circular, numbered one—and was pleased to see that I was still a good shot. I hadn't fired my piece in anger for a long time, but I was a hunter, after all, and in that game, you have to be sharp.

As I reloaded and fired again, I mulled over my plan. When Packman had finished shooting and was once again outside, I was going to approach and talk to him man to man, to tell him up front who I was and what I wanted to know. Sometimes it's best to play it straight and use direct confrontation.

I wanted to use Packman's innate temper against him, in much the same way a probing lawyer would incite a volatile witness on the stand, in the hope that their anger would get the better of them and they'd either blurt out the truth or at least useful information that the lawyer could then use to his or her advantage.

But would he talk to me? If he had nothing to

hide, then he'd have nothing to fear.

But if he did have something to hide, then not talking to me would make him seem guiltier. So, I figured, he'd talk to me either way—at least that's what I hoped.

Time dragged by, but eventually, after much spent ammo, he packed up, handed in his equipment, and headed outside to the parking lot.

When he reached his car and was just about to get his keys out, I made my move.

"Mr. Packman," I said with authority. "I'd like a moment of your time."

He turned towards me, confusion on his face.

"My name is Jack Valentine, I'm a private investigator working on the death of Brian Gates, can I ask you a couple of questions?"

"What, on a weekend, are you kidding me? I'm a busy man. I haven't got time for someone like you."

"I appreciate that Mr. Packman, but your close working relationship with Brian Gates puts you in a unique position to shed some light on—"

"—I got nothing to say, man!" he cut in. "They already got the guy who did it—Alfie Rose."

He shook his head dismissively, paused for a moment and then reacted as if a cartoon light bulb had pinged into existence above his head.

"Of course! That's who you're working for, right?"

"That's correct."

"Give it up Mr. Valentine, that kid is guilty and going down for it too: big public feud between him and 'The Gates,' admits he was present at the scene, even had Gates' blood on him, for heaven's sake!"

"I'm familiar with the details of the case, Mr. Packman. But of course, he wasn't the only one present at the scene, you attended the charity event yourself."

"Yeah, I was there, but that doesn't mean squat."

"Who was it you attended the event with that night?"

"I ain't speaking to you, hundreds of people attended, what does it matter who I was there with?"

"Hundreds did attend, but they didn't all argue with the deceased hours before his death."

"Say what?"

"I have solid information that you and Gates had a heated argument at the charity event. Is that true?"

"That is the biggest steaming pile of BS I've ever heard. Brian Gates and I were like brothers."

"Brothers who hated each other, you mean. Come on Mr. Packman, don't play the innocent with me, it was widely known that on a personal level you two couldn't stand each other."

"Not so."

"I think you knew he was planning to cut you off as his producer, and that's what the argument was about."

It was deer in the headlights time; Packman stood rooted to the spot, unable to prevent the flash of panic in his eyes. He was clearly taken aback that I knew this crucial detail.

I decided to take advantage: "That sort of betrayal must have cut deep, especially after all those years together, working as a team through it all. Even after your wife left you for him. I wouldn't blame you for wanting him six feet under."

Packman took the bait and exploded.

"Alright, you want me to tell you that I hated him? Well I did," he yelled. "You want me to tell you that I'm glad that no-good, double-crossing, scumbag is dead? Well I am. After everything I did for him, he deserved to die. Did you know it was me who gave him his big break on national television? He'd have been nothing without me. I made Brian Gates, not the other way around, and he stabbed me in the back. But, so what Mr. PI? You ain't got nothing on me, not a shred of evidence. So why don't you back the hell off, you hear me?!"

And with that, he got into his car, slammed the door, fired up the ignition, and hit the gas…

Bang!

His tire blew out, rendering it a limp, useless, flapping piece of rubber.

He jumped on the brakes and got out in a rage to survey the damage. I decided to leave him to it.

Getting in my own vehicle, I drove off past him with a wave, pondering the encounter and the man himself. That he had a temper was unquestionable.

He was impulsive, abusive and quick to anger—just the sort of person who could have lashed out and struck Brian Gates.

And by all accounts, he had reason to, and then some.

Packman was right about one thing though: as it stood, I didn't have anything on him, at least not solid evidence, and that's what counted.

I wasn't sure what my next move would be, but one thing was clear: I hadn't finished with Packman yet.

Not by a long shot.

CHAPTER 12

WINSTON, MY golden retriever, ran fast to my right, hair flowing in the breeze, such delight splashed across his face.

He ran with a seemingly wide grin, tongue flapping out of his mouth, chasing the stick like it was the prize he had worked his entire life for. I was jealous of him—to be that free, that open, is something I'll never experience; I've seen too much pain in my past, too much agony.

Not that Winston hadn't experienced pain—he adored Claire even more than I did. He didn't know what happened to her, he couldn't comprehend the hurt she experienced; he only knew that she was no longer there. Ignorance is bliss, so it would seem.

He did whimper for weeks after Claire's funeral, and I did everything I could to try and get rid of him. I didn't want a dog, especially one that reminded me of my deceased wife, but my friends didn't want him, Claire's family said no, and the pound was overfilled.

So, I was stuck with the mutt.

I heard once that you don't know love until you've raised a dog, and dammit, after all these years, they might be right.

Every day Winston finds his way into my heart just a little bit more.

Watching him run in the dog park—past the slow dogs, around the little ones, and barking at the loud ones—I have to say, I'm proud of him, and I'm proud that he's mine.

As much as he was Claire's, he's my boy now too.

Whenever we're at the park, Winston takes on his athletic persona. If he was human, he'd be a linebacker—all grunt, muscle, and adrenaline. I love that. I played linebacker in high school and a couple of college scouts came sniffing around after hearing about my aggression on the field. Unfortunately, in the game when three scouts arrived, I lost control and ripped someone's helmet off, before punching him into next week.

The kid shouldn't have said what he said about my mother, rest her soul, but I'll admit it, it was an over-reaction from me. The school thought so too and suspended me for the third time.

I had too much aggression, the scout's reports said, and they were probably right.

"Winston's moving well. Better than you ever could."

It was Derrick Booth; former cop, now retired, former smartass, still active, and owner of Barclay, a fellow golden retriever.

"At least I'm still moving, old man."

The bench at the east end of the fenced dog park

was basically owned by Derrick Booth. After his wife passed away ten years ago, he'd sat on the park bench more than he had at home. He was in his late seventies, a little overweight, and had the sort of face that looked like it had melted over time. He would've been handsome once, perhaps half a century ago, but time had wearied him, as it does all of us.

He was the centerpiece of this park, the social beacon, and I imagine that when his time came, someone would suggest that a plaque be placed on the bench in his honor.

"Been down to see Claire lately, Valentine?"

"She's resting well, thanks."

I sat down next to him. He had a thing for Claire, and she would often tell me about the nice old man that she talked to at the dog park. At her funeral, I saw him crying his eyes out. I guess that was sweet.

"Next time you're down at the grave, tell her I said hi." He grunted. "I'd get down there myself, but I can't travel far these days."

"I'm starting to think you had a crush on Claire."

"She was a lot sweeter than you."

"Thanks."

"And smarter."

"I get it."

"And so, so much better looking."

"No argument from me."

We sat next to each other on the bench for a moment of silence, taking in the sights. The park was almost empty with only two other dogs running around, along the grass that was patchy at best. The chain fence that surrounded the park wouldn't hold many dogs back, if they really wanted to run through it, and the trees looked almost lifeless, as if they were ready to fall down any moment.

"I saw you on the news, Valentine."

"I'm a popular guy."

"You working for the good guys yet?"

"If it's the good guys that want to find the truth, then sure. I'm working for Alfie Rose."

"Still the bad guys then." He shook his head.

"Girls love a bad boy."

"Maybe that's why Claire married you instead of me. I was too much of a good guy."

"Yeah, that's it."

"Give me the low down on the case, Valentine."

I could sense the excitement in his voice, as much as he tried to hide it. When you've spent the best part of forty years investigating crime, it's hard to leave it behind. And there was certainly no shortage of crime around here.

"I've got a kid who claims he's innocent, and a list of other potential killers as long as my arm. But there's evidence to say that the kid did it, and he certainly had a motive. Not looking good in the eyes of the court."

"Forget the court. They let killers walk free all the time." Spoken like a true cop. "Focus on what really happened, Valentine. Focus on the truth."

"I'm trying."

"Want to know my opinion?"

I shrugged. The real answer was 'not really,' but I listened to the old guy.

"I had a bit to do with that television world, in the days long before the internet. Even then, you could tell it was trouble. Death, corruption, and fraud were commonplace. It was almost like the mafia—run by these guys at the top. Some people just had too much power and it went to their heads. There's money in television, and that meant there's danger." He raised his finger. "If I had to put the house on a bet, I'd bet it was someone in the television industry."

"Doesn't help me."

He grunted, as if he had delivered a truck load of golden advice and I'd rejected it.

Derrick had helped me once before—I was struggling to crack a case of stolen milk, glamorous I know, and Claire begged me to take the file down to Derrick. I was hired by a supermarket who was missing a crate of milk every morning, and nobody could figure out how. They had installed cameras and the owner had spent nights on stakeouts, but still the milk was going missing. It was stumping me too, and I was starting to think that I should be taking the case to the X-Files instead of an old man on a park bench.

But I went with Claire's insistence and Derrick looked at the files, studied the photos for five minutes and pointed out that the supermarket was opposite a car yard. So what, I said. Cameras all down the street, he mentioned. Sure enough, he was right. And after getting the car yard to show us the footage, we saw that a group of grown men were entering a drain next to the car yard every night, and then exiting with a crate of milk. Turns out that the drain led to the underside of the cooler room in the back of the supermarket, and the men thought they could help themselves to whatever milk they wanted.

Sometimes, being a private investigator is about the little jobs, the small wins.

"Got a file for me to look at?" Derrick pressed.

"The case is in the courts and everything is confidential right now."

Derrick grunted again.

"I'll give you some advice for free, young man. To me, despite what the media has reported, despite what the prosecution is saying, this doesn't look like a planned murder. This looks like a moment of rage, a moment of lost control." He stood and whistled at Barclay. "So ask yourself, Valentine, which of your suspects could snap? Which of your suspects had the most potential to lash out, losing it in a moment of rage?"

I didn't answer, instead I looked out to the park and watched Winston chase Barclay.

But I'll give it to him, Derrick had asked a good question.

And it was one with a very easy answer.

CHAPTER 13

MY OFFICE door burst open.

Standing there with a look of indignation slapped across her makeup caked face, was an attractive, although stern looking, woman in an expensive tailor-made business suit, throwing her best steely expression my way. I'd never seen her before, but I had an idea who she was and what she wanted; in fact, I was surprised she hadn't made an appearance earlier.

"You're Jack Valentine?" The inflection in her voice sounded like she was less than impressed.

"I am."

She looked around my office, and she was even less impressed.

My office sat on the second floor off Clark St, in the Loop, near the Federal Prison. Not exactly prestigious, but not that bad either. The interior to my office was about as plain as it came. A football signed by the Bears sat on top of my bookshelf, and a baseball signed by the Cubs sat on the second shelf. There were three books on the middle shelf, only one of which I had read, and old sports magazines sat on the bottom shelf.

My Oakwood desk sat prominently in the dimly lit room; a computer monitor to one side, and a pile of files on the other side. The walls were exposed brick, which I liked, and the door was wooden, which I didn't like. The window let in enough sun to warm my back.

Outside my office, I had room for a secretary; a spare desk surrounded by a couple of dying potted plants; but I hadn't had a secretary in years. When Casey May, my assistant, came to the office, she would sit at that desk, although I wouldn't dare ask her to make me a coffee. Her death stare alone would cut me in two.

"My name is Betsy Jane, I'm the lead defense attorney for Mr. Alfie Rose," announced the woman, in the manner of a schoolteacher scolding a wayward pupil. "And your involvement in our case is not appreciated, nor in the best interests of my client."

My response was a sarcastic expression that begged the question: is that right?

From beneath my desk I pushed out the chair opposite with my foot.

"Take a seat, Betsy."

She strode over and sat down, leaning forward in the chair, fixing me once more with the same steely glare. It might have been intimidating to one of her first or second-year associates in the office, but with me, she was dealing with a completely different animal.

I'd faced down some seriously tough negotiators over the years—proper hardball players who knew the game and played for keeps—and I knew that I could top her, despite her reputation among the legal fraternity.

"Let's get one thing straight, up front," I said with authority. "Mr. Rose is my client, as well as your client. And if he has any complaints about the work he's commissioned me to do on his behalf, then that's for him to tell me, not you. Just as, if he has any complaints about the representation you're providing, then that's for him to tell you, not me. Understood?"

She gave a little nod, almost imperceptible but still there to see, betraying a small step backwards from her initial position. If negotiation was war, then she'd just retreated, and I'd advanced. She probably assumed that I'd be easily intimidated but standing up to her seemed to gain her respect.

"Okay, Valentine. The thing is," she said in a less confrontational tone. "My team and I have fought tooth and nail to get Alfie the deal the DOJ are offering up to him on a silver platter, and the reason Alfie's not taking the deal is simple: you've given him false hope; he thinks you're going to somehow wave a magic wand and prove the impossible, that he's as pure and innocent as the driven snow."

"By which, I take it, you're convinced of your own client's guilt?"

"That's a question I never answer, and, what's more, it's irrelevant to the professional representation

I provide, whether a client is innocent or guilty, they can expect a first class defense, which is what Alfie is getting from me, and my team. It's what we can prove in court that matters, what the jury can see and hear. And with this case, we're up against it. Trust me, I've been doing this a long time, and everything points to the jury returning a guilty verdict."

"Well, that's where you and I differ. I would expect a first-class defense to be fighting just as hard for a not guilty verdict. By the sounds of it you've already given up, thrown in the towel on his behalf after a few bumps in the road. Well, I haven't, not by a long shot. While there's breath still in me, I'll keep fighting for him. You see, I do believe Alfie is innocent, and what's more, I intend to prove it."

"That's a fallacy, Mr. Valentine," she said, shaking her head. "It's cloud cuckoo land nonsense, even for a man of your reputation, it's not going to happen. Saying something like that is easy, but actually following through and doing it is a very different matter altogether. Can't you see what you're doing to him? If Alfie turns down the DOJ's offer, which we both know is the best he's going to get, then the other most likely outcome is a life sentence for murder. How does that help him?"

"An innocent man isn't going to prison on my watch."

"Innocent? It doesn't matter who did it! That's irrelevant! What matters, what really matters, is what happens in that courtroom!" She was angry, but not with me. She was frustrated with herself, with her profession, knowing the words that came out of her mouth were as ridiculous as they sounded. "At this point in time, it doesn't look like he'll win. I don't know how much clearer I can make that to you. He'll go to prison for so much longer if this case goes to court. He has to agree to the deal."

"Alfie wouldn't last six months in the joint, let alone ten years, which, correct me if I'm wrong, is the best the DOJ is offering. He's dead either way, but if he takes their deal, you don't lose a case, at least not on paper, more like a negotiated draw, I'd say, so you leave with your reputation intact. I think that's what you're really worried about."

Her momentary silence and haste to change the subject confirmed that I was right.

"Mr. Valentine, I would encourage you to think beyond this individual case. I represent one of the biggest, most prestigious law firms in the city, clients of the highest order, many even bigger names than Mr. Rose. Should you take a step back from this particular case, then other opportunities could soon present themselves."

"I'm all ears."

"We deal with top end case after top end case and have an ongoing requirement for in-house investigators; investigators who get the highest level of work and are provided with the highest level of resources to complete that work. A man with a reputation like yours, well, he could lead a team like that.

"Is that right, and get the very best cases?"

"Sure, he could cherry pick his own, make an even bigger name for himself."

"Mmm. That is interesting. I imagine an investigator like that would need some pretty impressive office space to work out of."

"Oh, he'd get nothing but the finest prime real estate."

"Yes, I can see how that would be a golden opportunity, if you get my meaning."

"Yes, indeed, those yearly retainers, well, an investigator like that would be well looked after financially, in fact, he'd be a highly successful man."

"Yes, very interesting. Very interesting indeed."

She smiled confidently.

"There's only one snag," I said bluntly. "I'm not doing it."

Her smile turned first to surprise and then annoyance. She'd overplayed her hand and she knew it.

"You see for me it's all about the pursuit of justice."

"Let me speak frankly Mr. Valentine, I need you off the case and I'm willing to compensate you generously for your immediate withdrawal."

"I'm not interested."

"Whatever Mr. Rose is paying you, we'll double it."

"Double it, triple it, quadruple it, I'm not

interested. It's not about the money for me. If Alfie goes down, then justice isn't served. There'll be a miscarriage of justice, a big one, and soon after another murder, and probably a very gruesome one, only this time it will be Alfie's. Doesn't that mean anything to you? Have you not seen or read any of the death threats Alfie's been getting, laying out, step by step, how these sickos want to kill him, making it slow and painful?"

"Of course, I've read those notes, and I understand your concerns. But the fact remains, ten years is the best he's going to get, less with good behavior. It's a very generous offer, given the circumstances. At the end of the day, it's the prison system's responsibility to provide adequate protection to vulnerable inmates, and I have faith in the system to fulfil its obligations in that regard, especially given his high-profile status. He can survive in there. We can get him solitary confinement until the heat dies down. Alfie has nothing to worry about there, he'll be monitored and well looked after."

"Wow," I said, sitting back in my chair in amazement. "And you accuse me of living in cloud cuckoo land? That is some of the biggest BS I've ever heard in my life; and I've heard a lot, especially from lawyers… imagine that."

Her blasé disregard for Alfie had gotten my blood heated up now, she was putting him at risk for her own self-interest, and so I dropped any pretense at civility.

"You know, I'm not sure what worries me the most," I said. "That you might really believe what you just said, or that you don't believe it but are saying it regardless. Either way, Alfie is in dire trouble; if you don't believe it, then Alfie's got himself a lawyer who has zero concern for his wellbeing, so long as her reputation, and the reputation of her team, remains intact; and that they're well remunerated too, of course. But if you do believe it, then you've been spending too much time with the rest of the power suit set, cut off from the real world."

"I resent your fatuous insults, Mr. Valentine. Of course, I believe what I said. Just remember, I've been on this case a lot longer than you, doing the hard yards since the start, not coming along towards the end trying to scoop up the glory at the last minute."

"Now you listen and listen good. I was on the front line, pumping precious life back into Alfie's chest after the attempt on his life, while you were doing what? Probably having fancy business lunches at the Four Seasons with your friends at the DOJ, scarfing down foie gras and truffles, while quaffing three hundred-dollar glasses of Chateau Latour—and billing your client for the privilege, no doubt."

"Trust me. That's not how it works."

"Oh, I've seen how it works. And I've seen what happens to the Alfies of this world in prison. Don't believe the PR spin: Prisons aren't run by the book but by the crook, lots of them, all struggling inside for their own power and advantage. It's multi-layered, with everybody fighting for their little bit, no matter how small or far down the chain they are. Throats are cut and skulls are cracked for sport. There's always going to be some wannabe looking to build their reputation, and Alfie's going to be the perfect target. I'm telling you straight: if Alfie goes to prison, he will die there. I've seen it many times—and there wasn't ever a heroic prison guard stepping in to ensure fair play—I sure as hell don't want to see it happen here. You need to fight for Alfie, just like I'm doing, build a not guilty case, because that's what he is."

"Don't tell me how to do my job. I've won case after case and worked tirelessly for the DOJ offer that you and Alfie seem determined to squander. I'll let you know, I'm a former Harvard law professor, one of the most respected and powerful lawyers in Chicago, not some two-bit PI working out of a glorified closet."

"Well, as Margret Thatcher once said, being powerful is like being a lady... if you have to tell people you are, you aren't."

"It seems I'm wasting my time," she said, standing up from the desk. "I had hoped you'd be able to see some sense, to see that not only is the DOJ offer the best offer Alfie is going to get, but that it's the only offer he's going to get; in fact, it's the only realistic option he has. Everything else is a dead end. If you insist on pursuing your own fantasy of cracking this case wide open then that's up to you, but I resent what you've done to our case and, by extension, Mr.

Rose."

"And I resent that a good man like Alfie Rose finds himself with such a highly educated fool for his leading defense council."

She turned and marched out the door, slamming it on the way out.

I sat back in my chair and lit a cigarette, inhaling deeply.

As meetings go it was hardly a success, but it wasn't entirely unproductive either. It hit home something I already knew: I needed to redouble my efforts, to step it up another gear. Alfie's only hope was me. His trial was around the corner, and it was too late for him to switch defense teams now. He was saddled with what he had: a defense team who was more interested in defending their reputation than their client, fighting for a draw.

When I fought, it was only ever to win.

But I needed to fight quickly.

And it was time now to fight dirty.

CHAPTER 14

I GLANCED at the clock on the office wall: nearly midnight.

Fatigue ate away at me, testing my resolve to continue, gnawing away at my purpose, tempting me with beguiling images of rest. I was running on empty, eking out the last of the dirty fuel of caffeine and nicotine in my tank. I sloshed another serving of coffee into my mug and gulped it down like bad tasting medicine, desirous of effect on my body not sensation on my palate.

I'd been working on a link chart on my bulletin board; you know, those charts you see on the television cop shows where detectives investigating a crime pin pictures of people, locations, cars etc., with lines linking one picture to another. They're a great way of connecting people and evidence with visual links—my personal preference for processing information. They come into their own during complex longitudinal investigations, with multiple players, addresses—both physical and IP—telephone numbers, vehicles and so on.

In the center of my chart was a photo of Brian

Gates, the same cheesy publicity shot that had been used at his memorial, taken from a program I'd acquired on that day. The links coming from it were mindboggling, like the spectrum of rays emanating from the sun: woman after woman, after woman; one big, happy, merry-go-round of infidelity, spreading out to the four corners of my wall.

An intermingling spaghetti junction of jilted husbands added to the complexity, as did aggrieved former work colleagues, those who benefitted in some way from his death, and vocal critics in the media.

I'd been adding information on Packman, new intel that Casey had dug up in the last twenty-four hours, business deals he'd done with production companies, and proposed deals he'd penciled in with networks, which, had Brian Gates jumped ship and gone it alone without him, would have been dead. There was big money involved, but unless Brian was part of the program too, it was all null and void.

Money is one almighty motivator and the loss of it likewise, but money comes and goes; it seemed obvious to me from Packman's reaction to my enquiries that betrayal, and quite possibly jealousy, was as much, if not more, of a factor in his hatred towards Gates than financial loss. Gates had everything Packman secretly desired: all the adulation, all the fame, all the column inches talking about him, even all the controversy, and certainly all the women.

Packman on the other hand, got his share of the

money, which, as a producer, was substantial. But it wasn't enough. No, it seemed to me that Packman fancied himself in Gates' shoes, and in his deluded mind probably even believed he could do what Gates did, as the anchor man in front of the camera, not the unsung producer behind it.

Everyone knew Gates, but for Packman, outside of the little media production bubble in which he worked, nobody knew him.

I stared at the link chart, following the lines from one person to the other, slightly letting go of conscious thought, letting my subconscious wander freely in the hope it would pick something up that I had missed.

It didn't happen.

I was flagging, I needed rest to be effective and decided to turn in for the night. There was no point pushing on, lest I miss something that a clear head after sufficient sleep would spot in the morning.

I grabbed my coat and headed outside, breathing in the surprisingly cool night air, summer was in full swing, but you wouldn't know it tonight. It was cold and windy, but it perked me up as I walked along the street toward the "L" station, making my way past the radiance of downtown bars with their raucous patrons breathing life into the night, and ubiquitous late night food joints, tempting me to stop with aromas of juicy meats and hot sauces. I was hungry, but more for rest than sustenance. Bed was calling my name, and it wouldn't be denied.

It was a short walk to the station, and only five minutes wait on the platform before I boarded the sleep-inducing warmth of the first train car. It was occupied by drunks celebrating in their myriad forms: the happy incoherent babbler, the silent wall-staring depressive, and everybody's favorite, the aggressive foul-mouthed shouter.

I was tempted by a moment's shuteye, but the yelling emanating from the foul-mouthed shouter at the far end of the car had me remaining awake instead, just in case he got physically aggressive with someone and I had to administer my own brand of sleeping medication for him, in the form of a solid right hander to the jaw. It wouldn't be the first time on a late-night journey home, but he got off soon after without incident, and by the time I arrived at my stop I was exhausted.

Moments later I was outside my apartment, fumbling in my pocket for my keys when the door of a car parked outside opened up onto the sidewalk.

From inside came the most improbable sound.

"Mr. Valentine, I'd like a word, off the record," said a husky female voice.

From my position it was impossible to see who it was, but the voice was familiar. I approached the car slowly, and there, sitting inside alone, was none other than Lizzie Guthrie.

"Hello, Jack," she smiled up at me, flashing a perfect set of Hollywood-white teeth.

"Lizzie, how long have you been here?"

"Too long, and it's freezing. Are you going to invite a girl in from the cold, or what?"

I paused momentarily, wondering what it was all about, what she wanted, what her motives were, and the implications.

There was only one way to find out.

"Sure, come in," I said, holding the door open as she stepped out of the car.

We made our way inside, through the lobby to the elevator. We stood in silence for it to arrive, then rode it side by side to my floor without a word shared between us. It was too late for chit chat, if she wanted to talk then she could. As for me, I was waiting for her to make the first move.

When we reached my apartment and stepped inside, she turned my way and touched me tenderly on the arm, staring at me with her big blue eyes.

"Can a girl get a drink?"

"Sure, coffee?"

"I was thinking whiskey."

"Ice?"

"Two rocks."

I fetched her drink and poured myself one too: double shot, neat.

She took a slow sip and held my attention once more with those big saucer eyes.

"You look like you've got the weight of the world on your shoulders, Jack," she said softly, rubbing her hand up my forearm. "Let me help lift it."

I didn't respond.

She took a step closer and leaned in towards my ear.

"I saw someone at the charity event outside Brian Gates' dressing room," she whispered.

I took a step back, so she was at arm's length and looked her squarely in the eye without warmth.

"What's the matter Jack, why are you no fun?" she said with a disappointed huff.

"It's too late for games, Lizzie. You got something for me? Well, let's hear it. Otherwise…"

I glanced towards the door.

"Come on, Jack," she said. "You know I've always had a soft spot for you, don't shut me out."

She looked me in the eye again, and for a second I thought she might try her luck once more, but she could see I wasn't biting. She wasn't the sort of woman used to getting rejected, to not getting her own way, but I wasn't the sort of man to be toyed with, not by her, nor anyone else.

With a reluctant sigh, she backed off.

"It was Packman," she stated, matter-of-factly.

"You're sure about that?"

"As sure as you're standing here."

"What was he doing, going in or coming out?"

"Going in, looking mighty upset."

"And what were you doing near there?"

"Oh, Brian and I liked to 'chat' from time to time," she said, raising an eyebrow. "I'm sure you know how it is."

"Chat, hey? Oh, I'm sure he was a great

conversationalist."

"Actually Jack, he was, among other things."

"And what time was this?"

"About ten forty-five."

"You realize this makes you a suspect as much as it does Packman, eleven o'clock is the estimated time of death."

"Sure, but then this is off the record, Jack. Anyone tries to get me to testify to this and I'll deny it completely, no question about that. I never said a word of this or anything like it to you, it's all just a figment of your overactive imagination, don't you know? The only person that knew I was there, is… well, he can't testify at his own murder trial."

"Understood but being at the scene at that very time implicates you just as much as him."

"Really? You think I moved the body? What, a slender size eight like me?" she said, suggestively tracing her hands down from her tiny waist to her hips. "Whereas big, butch, muscly Pat, of course…"

She had a point.

Whoever killed Brian Gates had moved his body, forensics had established that, and Brian Gates was a big man, well over 200 pounds, as was Packman.

"And you're telling me this why, Lizzie? Out of the goodness of your heart, I suppose?"

"Brian and I were closer than you might imagine. Brian really saw me, understood me, in a way that people would struggle to believe. I want his killer punished. They stole a great man from this planet, a man of warmth, humor and genuine passion, someone I miss and the world is a poorer place without, is that so hard to believe?"

"So why the silence until now, until the trial of Alfie Rose is just about to begin? Why didn't you tell the police this when their investigation started? This could have been a significant line of inquiry, but instead you tell me, off the record, why?"

"Why do you think?" she said, flashing her wedding ring my way. "You think Hugh and I want the world to know our business, what's between us and no one else. If I admit to my relationship with Brian then it would be all over the gutter press; they'd have a field day, front page coverage on every tabloid, racking up every bit of salacious dirt for their own voyeuristic pleasure and profit."

"That's true enough, and if what you're telling me is true, then it's significant."

She smiled, giving me those eyes again and stepping closer.

"Of course it's true. I just want to help, Jack. We've always had a connection, you and me. We'd make a good team, you know. How about it?"

She reached towards me, but I checked her arm.

"Lizzie, you don't even know me. I worked for Hugh one time, briefly. And we met, what, a handful of times?"

"If it's Hugh that bothers you."

"What?"

"We have an arrangement. I'm not his keeper and

neither is he mine."

"Let me be clear. There is no connection, it's a wrong number. Completely disconnected."

She looked hurt but I hit home the point.

"In fact, I'm not even sure the phone is on."

Down went her drink onto the nearby sideboard.

She started to leave but then turned to me as if about to say something, only to think better of it at the last minute. She shook her head with clear annoyance instead, turned on her heel and strode off into the night, back to Hugh, maybe, or heaven knows where. It didn't matter to me. What did, was her information. But was it credible? Did she really see Packman outside Gates' dressing room at the time of his murder? And if so, why was she really telling me?

I didn't doubt that her marriage vows to Hugh were interpreted loosely, but it seemed likely she had some ulterior motive for spilling the beans other than love for the deceased.

I was still tired, but now also restless, questions running around my mind unchecked. I'd be taking Lizzie Guthrie to bed alright, but not in the manner she wanted. She'd be on my mind as I lay there trying to sleep, wondering what it all meant, and, more importantly, what my next move was. Whatever it was, it would have to be decisive. Alfie's trial began in less than a week, and his life, more than ever, depended on how I proceeded tactically over the next few days.

Packman was already in my sights. And with the new information from Lizzie, I was now practically ready to pull the trigger.

CHAPTER 15

A BLEACHED blond teenager with a classic 'angry girl haircut' of super short wonky-lined fringe that revealed nearly all of her forehead, knelt on the cold stone steps leading up to the courthouse, wailing at the top of her lungs into the unresponsive air, as if the world as she knew it was about to end at any moment.

The media circus was lapping it up, paparazzi cameras flashing all over the place to capture the melodramatic image, while film crews got their rushes for the evening news.

"What does Alfie Rose mean to you?" yelled a reporter to the kneeling hysteric.

"Alfie is the world's most innocent man. He is a kind, big hearted, gentle giant. I love him. I would die for Alfie Rose!"

She pumped her fist triumphantly into the air.

"Yeah! Me too!" yelled another Rose groupie nearby.

"Me too!"

"Yeah, me as well!"

Competition for Alfie's greatest, or most deranged,

fan was on alright, and there was no shortage of participants, with a large collection congregated by their kneeling comrade.

"If they convict him, I will kill myself," screamed the girl on her knees, raising the stakes even further.

The others echoed her sentiment, although this time not quite so enthusiastically.

What happened next was beyond my comprehension.

From the girl's jacket pocket came a canister of pepper spray, which she held aloft.

"In the Sixties a Buddhist monk became an icon by burning himself alive in protest at the Vietnam War," she screamed. "This is our generation's Vietnam! This is for Alfie!" she paused briefly, checking the nozzle was aimed the right way and then, while everyone was staring open-mouthed at her in disbelief, let it rip with the canister, squirting herself in the face with a big orange covering of capsicum.

"Ahhhh!!!!!" she screamed, as the spray took effect.

Even her fellow groupies looked shocked at that one.

Ladies and Gentlemen, I thought to myself, I think we have a winner.

I left the bonkers brigade to it and made my way up the steps towards the courthouse, passing some Brian Gatesers yelling at two teenagers wearing t-shirts emblazoned with the words: Alfie's Angels.

"Innocent, is he? That no-good killer is gonna die

like a dog!"

"Yeah, let him fry!" yelled another.

At the top of the steps was another group of Alfie devotees, who had formed a rather ineffective human barrier.

"Don't cross our picket line!" announced several of their signs.

It, like most everything else outside the courthouse, made little sense to me, as if they were trying to block access to the court then they had failed miserably on two fronts: firstly, everyone of any importance was already inside; and secondly, their line was nowhere near the building's actual front door, allowing me to stride on inside uninterrupted, which is exactly what I did.

A few preliminary security checks and I was shown through the expansive lobby to the courtroom itself.

Despite strenuous protest from his lawyers, Alfie had put me down as a person of importance, allowing me to skip the usual pretrial lines for a spot in the packed public gallery. I made the decision to spend the first few days of the trial in court, looking for any clue I might've missed. I needed the thinking time, and I needed the time to piece it all together. Casey was out doing the investigative leg work on the streets, and I could help after the day in court.

Taking a seat at the back of the courtroom, I looked around. Supporters of the accused and the deceased packed the gallery, with court reporters, journalists and family members of Rose and Gates making up the rest. A nervous looking Alfie sat up front with his legal team; and across from them, the prosecution's big gun lawyers, hard hitters every one of them, who looked ready for a fight, the months of preparation finally over and the battle about to begin. The place buzzed with anticipation, a nervous tension pervading the court to the extent that even the seasoned security staff looked on edge.

It was clear something very big was going down today.

"All rise. Cook County Criminal Court is now in session. The Honorable Judge Clifton presiding."

In walked the judge, Norris Clifton, a no nonsense, conservative, law and order merchant, whose lack of empathy and personal power trips were legendry. A guilty verdict with Clifton meant the maximum sentence, every time.

He took his time to sit, plumping up and then repositioning a big comfy cushion on his chair.

When finally satisfied, he instructed the bailiff to welcome the jury. They were Alfie's supposed twelve peers, the men and women whom his fate resided in. I took a good look at them one by one, wondering about their selection process, their prejudices, and their ability to base their verdict on the evidence, and the evidence alone. Problem was, the evidence was strong.

"Good morning ladies and gentlemen of the jury," Judge Clifton stated. "We are going to begin with the opening statements made by the lawyers in the case.

As I explained to you yesterday, these statements are not to be considered evidence. They are an overview of the type of evidence that the attorneys intend to present to you."

He turned to the lawyers.

"Are both sides ready to proceed?"

"We are, Your Honor."

"Yes, Your Honor."

"Then proceed, we shall."

First up was the prosecution's statement, delivered by their lead attorney, Christine McIntyre.

I'd seen McIntyre in action before and she was no joke. In fact, she was quietly terrifying.

A small woman in stature but with a giant presence, she was the classic wolf in sheep's clothing, who you underestimated at your peril, as many had before and then perished. She had a killer instinct, an encyclopedic knowledge of the law, was a superb tactician and a captivating speaker who could tie even the best prepared defendants up in mental knots.

She loved, thrived in and understood the theater of the law. But what made her cross examinations especially intimidating was her strategic use of silence, those awkward moments in-between questions and answers where she would pause, sometimes agonizingly long, leaving defendants as exposed and vulnerable as newborn lambs without a mother. And this wolf had no mercy.

She made her way to the front of the court.

"Your Honor, Judge Clifton, my colleagues seated

here before you today, and to the people most interested in the outcome of this case: The Gates family, and the Rose family, and of course to you, ladies and gentlemen of the jury, good morning."

She took a few paces, looking from juror to juror, letting her presence fill the silence of the room.

"Thou. Shalt. Not. Kill."

She said it slowly but firmly, one word at a time, letting the gravity of her words sink in.

"It's been the ultimate crime since the beginning of humanity, the taking of another human life. You steal a wallet, a car, some jewelry, they can be replaced, claimed on your insurance, if you're lucky enough to have some, but a life? No. No one can give that back."

She paused again and looked the foreman of the jury in the eye.

"No one."

She shook her head with a look of regret.

"Not me, not the judge, and not you. No matter what happens over the course of this trial, and what the outcome is, no one can bring back the life of Brian Gates. That's what makes my job so difficult, and what makes your job so hard. But both our jobs have a central focus and a clear objective. That objective is justice. To deliver justice, we need to answer a question. It's a question that I'm sure most everyone has been asking, all across this great country. That question is, did Alfie Rose kill Brian Gates?"

She turned towards Alfie and eyeballed him while she said it, practically staring him down until he squirmed in his seat.

She was good, really good, and the jury looked impressed and enthralled.

"Well ladies and gentlemen, I stand here in front of you today to answer that question, through credible witness testimony, DNA analysis, and of course through unequivocal hard evidence. It will make it easy, simple even, for when you piece everything together, there is only one answer.

The answer is: Yes, Alfie Rose murdered Brian Gates.

My name is Christine McIntyre, and with my team, we will present to you an astounding amount of evidence that will leave you with no doubt about the guilt of Alfie Rose.

Mr. Brian Gates was a respected newscaster, whose career had spanned decades across numerous networks, and whose opinion was respected throughout this city, and throughout the country.

Mr. Alfie Rose is a professional gamer, a young man that earns his money from playing computer games online.

That profession annoyed Mr. Gates, and he announced that opinion loudly, and often. Mr. Gates belittled Mr. Rose, his profession, and his personality.

Throughout this trial, you will hear from witnesses that will tell you that Mr. Rose had said that he had enough of Mr. Gates' attacks, that he was going to put a stop to the abuse.

And he certainly did that.

He ended it for good.

Mr. Rose murdered Mr. Gates in cold blood in his dressing room after a charity function. Mr. Gates died as a result of a brutal blow to his head, delivered by the large and aggressive Mr. Rose.

Mr. Gates spent his last hours raising money for others. He was raising money for charity, doing good in this world, and it ended up costing his life.

Over the coming weeks, we will present numerous witnesses to you that will explain there is no reasonable doubt, no doubt, that Mr. Rose caused the death of Mr. Gates, and that he had intended to do so.

By the end of this trial, you will understand that Mr. Rose had the intention to cause death. He had the intention to murder Mr. Gates. He knew that what he did would end Mr. Gates' life.

You will hear from witnesses that will explain the hatred that Mr. Rose had for Mr. Gates, stemming from the fact that Mr. Gates had attacked Mr. Rose verbally, not only on that night, but also in the months previous. The witnesses will explain to you how those verbal attacks started to eat away at Mr. Rose, started to get under his skin, until he decided that he had enough. Mr. Rose had decided that he was going to defend himself from these verbal attacks, and he was going to do so physically.

He decided that he was going to murder Mr.

Gates.

You will hear from witnesses that were also attending the charity function that fateful night, and they will explain to you how angry Mr. Rose was after Mr. Gates continued to verbally attack him throughout the night. Mr. Gates made a speech, and throughout the speech, he made jokes about Mr. Rose, personally and professionally. Are jibes enough of a reason to cause someone's death? The defense team may ask you that question, and they will ask you to consider whether Mr. Rose was defending himself. Looking at you, the jurors, I can see that you won't be tricked by these questions.

Throughout this trial, you will also hear from witnesses that will state that they saw Mr. Rose enter Mr. Gates' dressing room after the function.

Dr. Christopher Payne, a chief medical examiner, will explain that he performed the autopsy on Mr. Gates and he will detail the estimated time of death, along with the cause of death. He will present his autopsy report and detail the photos he took of Mr. Gates' deceased body. This may be upsetting to you, however, it will help you grasp the callous and disgusting nature of this crime.

Detectives from the Chicago Police Department involved in the case will also explain how they investigated the death and arrested and charged Mr. Rose with first degree murder within a matter of days. They will explain the evidence that they gathered in those days, and they will detail how they came to the conclusion that Mr. Rose was guilty of murder. They will explain to you what Mr. Rose said after he was arrested, including the statement that Mr. Rose admitted being in that dressing room only moments before Mr. Gates died.

They will present the arrest report to you and explain it in detail.

You will hear from a DNA expert, who will explain how Mr. Gates' blood was found on the sleeve of Mr. Rose's shirt.

You will hear from experts who will detail the crime scene and explain how Mr. Rose attempted to move Mr. Gates' body after he murdered him.

You will hear from a long list of witnesses, people who all have evidence about this case, and they will all confirm that you can only come to one… one… conclusion.

When these witnesses have finished providing their testimonies, you will have no reasonable doubt that Mr. Rose intended to kill Mr. Gates, and he did so that night.

There's a lot of noise surrounding this case. There's a lot of hatred out there, for both sides of the argument. There are very vocal people voicing their opinions about the murder, and this case is in the news.

But you cannot, you cannot, let that noise influence your decisions.

Your decisions here, in this court, must be without bias, without prejudgment, and without outside influence. The defense team will spin a fanciful tale; one full of mistruths, and misdirection. Don't be fooled by their theories. Don't be fooled by their tricks. You must look through their games, through the stories, and you must only see the evidence.

You must listen to the facts, listen to the proof, and after you have done so, you will only come to one conclusion.

Only one.

And that conclusion will be that Mr. Alfie Rose is guilty of the first-degree murder of Mr. Brian Gates.

Thank you for your service to this court."

It was an impressive performance, one worthy of a Broadway theater, and I almost felt like standing to applaud, but as she finished her statement, my phone buzzed on silent.

It was a message from Casey: New info on Packman, meet me in the park outside.

I slipped out quietly, exiting the courthouse, making my way down the steps and across the road to the park, where Casey was waiting with a file in one hand and an optimistic smile on her face.

"How'd it go?" she asked.

"Not good. McIntyre was on fire. Had the jury in the palm of her hand."

"Doesn't she always?"

"Yeah, she's good all right. So, what've you got for me?"

"Police file on Packman, wasn't easy to get, but well worth the effort."

She handed it over.

"Take a look, he's got a previous conviction for… violent assault."

"Interesting. Very, very interesting."

"And by all accounts should have another conviction too. Apparently three years ago he had a difference of opinion with a work colleague and lashed out at him, punched the man unconscious. There were witnesses but the victim refused to press charges. Rumor has it, Packman either paid him off or threatened him with more of the same if he proceeded. Either way, the guy backed off, and Packman got away scot free."

"Good Job, Casey. This is gold."

"Thanks."

"Any news on Lizzie Guthrie?"

"Not yet, she's my next priority."

"Do whatever it takes and let me know how it goes."

"Will do."

"I'm gonna run, see if I can get back before the first witness."

"Best of luck, and send my regards to the kid," said Casey, heading off towards her car.

As I made my way up the courthouse steps, my phone buzzed again.

"Laura." I answered. "I don't really have time for-"

"Don't talk to me about time, Jack." She snapped. "I've just talked to the doctor. She says things are happening with the cancer quicker than she expected.

I need to know who did it, Jack. Before I go, you need to find me the answer. Someone has to be held responsible for my daughter's death."

I paused and sighed. There was no use arguing with her. "Yes, ma'am."

"And Jack?"

"Yes?"

She took a moment. "Thank you."

She hung up the phone without another word.

I drew a deep breath, pushed Laura to the back of my mind, and continued my walk through security.

By the time I arrived back in the courthouse there was a recess. The defense had made their opening statement, and people were milling around in the corridors outside. Sitting on a bench alone, slumped over with his head in his hands was the figure of Alfie Rose.

"Don't worry, son," I said in my best positive voice.

"Jack!" he said, with a smile. "Am I pleased to see you."

"That was quick. What happened, judge need a bathroom break?"

"If only. A fight broke out in court. A protester started yelling and threw a shoe at me, only they missed and hit McIntyre in the back of the head."

"You're joking."

"Nah, she looks alright though."

Alfie gestured down the corridor, where McIntyre, along with the rest of the prosecution, were discussing something with Alfie's defense team. It looked all too cozy to me, like they were still angling for a plea deal, not fighting for his innocence. I'd missed the defense's opening statement, but after my encounter with Betsy Jane, I didn't have much faith in her abilities to counteract the formidable McIntyre.

Alfie frowned. By the looks of it, he was concluding much the same himself.

"Hey, this'll cheer you up," I said, hoping a bit of gallows humor would lighten the mood. "There's a man on trial in court, and the judge says to him, 'You are charged with beating your wife to death with a hammer,' and a voice from the back of the court yells, 'You lowlife!' and it all goes quiet, like. And the judge says, 'You are also charged with beating your dog to death with a hammer,' and the voice from the back of the court yells 'You scumbag!' And the judge says, 'Well this can't go on.' He pulls the man in front of him and says, 'Now look, I can understand you being a bit upset about this case, but if there are any more outbursts like this, I shall charge you will contempt. Now what's the problem?' And the man says, 'Well, I lived next door to him for over thirty years... and every time I asked to borrow a hammer, he said he didn't have one!'"

Alfie laughed, so I hit him with another.

"There's another man in court charged with stealing an overcoat, and the judge says to him 'Weren't you before me four years ago for stealing an overcoat?' and the man replies… 'Well how long do you think an overcoat lasts?"'

Alfie laughed again, but I didn't continue.

I had more jokes up my sleeve, but it could be a long trial and I didn't know when I might need them later.

The first prosecution witness was about to give evidence next, and, by all accounts, it seemed likely to be one hell of a damning testimony.

CHAPTER 16

DETECTIVE O'REILLY stood in the witness stand, practically filling it with his herculean size. He was an impressive man, 6 foot 4 inches and over 250 pounds of muscle, one of Chicago's finest, and decorated several times, twice for extreme bravery.

We'd only met the once, at my brother-in-law's wedding, where O'Reilly had been the best man. We hadn't spoken much on that day, at least not beyond the normal pleasantries you exchange with strangers at such events; you know, a quick 'Hello,' 'How do you know the couple?' 'What sort of work do you do?' and then on to the next person.

He'd struck me as an uber confident individual, but that changed when I saw him in front of a crowd. Despite his imposing size, he wasn't the best public speaker, in fact, if his best man speech at the wedding was anything to go by, then he was downright bad at it. But delivering a captivating and witty wedding speech to a couple of hundred guests is very different than answering the sort of factual questions he seemed likely to be asked today, which would be relating to what was, ultimately, his forte: police work.

I wasn't certain how he would perform on the stand, but I hoped he'd display the same sort of nerves and indecisiveness I'd witnessed at the wedding, and that Alfie's defense would tear a hole in him, but as he took the oath, introduced himself and settled in for the prosecution's first question, my hopes faded. He looked calm, confident and at ease. It was hardly a surprise; this was, after all, effectively another day in the office for him, and something he must have done a hundred times before in the line of duty.

"Officer O'Reilly, would you tell the court your role at the Chicago Police Department?" asked Prosecutor McIntyre.

"I'm a major crimes investigator for the crime scenes unit, specializing in homicide investigations. I've proudly served this city, and this community, for more than two decades."

"And it was your investigation, was it not, that led to the arrest of the accused?"

"Yes, Ma'am, it was."

"Talk me through the morning you found the dead body of Brian Gates, will you please, Detective O'Reilly?"

"Well, Ma'am, I was the first police officer on the scene after an emergency call was placed by the venue's manager, alerting us to a body, which was found by a member of his cleaning staff the morning after a charity event that was hosted by the deceased, Mr. Brian Gates. I arrived at roughly 8am on the morning of the twelfth of January and found Brian Gates' body face down in his dressing room, congealed blood emanating from a significant wound to the back of his head. His body was cold, indicating that he died some time earlier."

"You've been a police officer for a long time, haven't you Officer O'Reilly?"

"Yes, Ma'am, twenty-two years and counting."

"Would it be fair to say that you've witnessed a lot of dead bodies over the years in the course of your work?"

"Too many, but yes, I have."

"Do you have a lot of experience in this area?"

"I do."

"And in your experience, what was your first impression of the scene?"

"My first impression was that something didn't look right, and on closer inspection it wasn't right."

"In what way?"

"Things looked like they'd been moved around in the dressing room after the event, after the murder had taken place."

"What sort of things?"

"Furniture had been moved, but the most obvious thing was the body itself. As I said, I've seen a lot of dead bodies over the years and when a person falls, they do so in a certain manner that has an authenticity about it, which is sometimes difficult to categorize but easy to recognize, especially in its unauthenticity. If a body has been moved by an amateur and repositioned to look 'natural,' then the trained eye of a professional can often pick it up, sometimes at a glance. Brian Gates' body was, and I apologize to his family for using this word, comically repositioned, almost spread eagle, with arms and legs out in all directions. Most often a person who is struck by a fatal blow crumples in an awkward manner, normally on top of a limb or two, not in a nice neat Hollywood movie kind of way."

"Was there anything else about the scene that didn't seem right to you, in your experience?"

"Yes, there were remnants of what looked like smear marks, where someone had tried to wipe away blood from certain areas."

"What areas?"

"Chairs, only the person who did it didn't do a very thorough job. They'd left big smears there, highlighting, inadvertently, the fact they'd tampered with the scene."

"And as the investigating officer, your enquiries led you to the accused, to Mr. Alfie Rose, didn't they?"

"Yes, they did."

"Would you please tell the court why?"

"Well to begin with, Alfie Rose was the last person to see Brian Gates alive…"

"…Objection, your honor," piped up Alfie's defense council. "This is pure speculation on the officer's part."

"Sustained," agreed the judge.

"Withdrawn," responded McIntyre, "May it please Your Honor, for Officer O'Reilly to tell the court what led him to believe that Mr. Rose was the last person to see Brian Gates alive."

"I'll allow it but tread carefully Officer."

"Well," continued Officer O'Reilly, "Mr. Rose admitted to entering the dressing room at around twenty-two hundred hours, 10pm, and despite rigorous inquiries that were carried out by myself and several of my officers, not one person, be they venue staff or fellow attendees of the event, reported seeing anyone else remotely near Brian Gates' dressing room at that time. However, many people report seeing Alfie Rose. Had another individual been there after Rose, it is highly likely someone would have seen them. And the estimated time of death is around 11pm on the night of the charity event, with a degree of leeway either side, so it matches well. Especially given that Rose admits going into the dressing room to confront the deceased…"

"Objection!" said Betsy Jane, rising again to her feet. "My client admits to entering the dressing room, but only to talk to Brian Gates, to smooth things over, not to 'confront him' as Officer O'Reilly so casually asserts with zero evidence, and certainly with no recorded testimony or statements from Mr. Rose, which remotely back up this erroneous claim. If Mr. Rose has ever made a statement to that effect then I, for one, would like to hear it."

The judge turned to McIntyre and O'Reilly.

"Officer O'Reilly and council for the prosecution, do you know of any testimony from Mr. Rose in which he specifically states he entered the dressing room to, in Officer O'Reilly's words, 'confront' Mr. Gates?"

"We do not, Your Honor," replied a fleetingly contrite McIntyre.

"Then members of the jury are to disregard Officer O'Reilly's last statement that Alfie Rose entered the dressing room with the intention of confronting Brian Gates. Whether or not that was the case is, obviously, to be determined in the course of this trial itself, but it is not for the officer to state an opinion as if it were a fact. I hope that is understood, Officer O'Reilly."

"It is. I apologize, Your Honor."

"Please continue, but just the facts as they happened."

"The point I was going to make is, no matter how long their verbal exchange took, it would confirm they were together at the same location at a time even closer to, or right in line with, the ETOD—sorry, estimated time of death."

"I'd like to turn to the blood…" said McIntyre. "…Brian Gates' blood."

She paused, emphasizing the last bit while looking over at the jury.

"You mentioned earlier that Brian Gates' blood had been wiped off the chairs, but had been left elsewhere, can you please elaborate?"

"Yes, blood had been wiped from the chairs but not the carpet, as if someone was trying to conceal something, and by the looks of the trail of blood on the carpet, the body had been dragged a significant distance towards a table."

"And was there anything unusual about the table?"

"Yes, there was. The corner of the table had been dabbed with blood, clearly applied with something other than the impact of a head."

"What did it look like to you?"

"Like someone had dabbed the corner of the table with a bloodied cloth."

"Why?"

"It's hard to say with any certainty, but it appeared to be a panicked and amateurish attempt to make it look like a fall, as if Brian Gates had tripped and hit his head on the corner of the table, and that his injuries and the blood left there were the result of that, as opposed to being battered by a bottle of champagne."

"And, in your experience, is that scenario possible, given what you witnessed at the scene?"

"No. The whole scene had been tampered with, and not remotely in a convincing manner. To me it looks like the murderer had a silly idea to mess with the evidence but then at some point realized it wasn't working and decided to hightail it out of there instead."

"So, whoever did this would likely have got some of Brian Gates' blood on them too?"

"Yes, given the quantity of blood at the scene, even if the person responsible was extremely careful, it would be virtually impossible for them not to get some blood on themselves. In fact, I'd say quite a bit of blood."

Prosecutor McIntyre looked from Officer O'Reilly to the jury, highlighting its importance.

"And did you discover any of Brian Gates' blood anywhere other than his dressing room?"

"Yes, Ma'am we did."

"And where was that?"

"All over the clothing of Alfie Rose."

"All over?" she asked, looking once more towards the jury.

"Yes, there was a lot. On his shirt. On his pants. Even on his shoes."

An older woman on the jury cringed.

McIntyre was looking straight at the juror and played directly to her for effect, hitting home the point.

"Even on his shoes. It sounds like he was almost…" she paused again for theatrical tension "… soaked in blood!"

"Objection, your honor!" Alfie's defense jumped up once more. "This is a wholly inaccurate expression to use. It paints an unfair and untrue picture of the amount of blood recovered from the items. I'm sure council for the prosecution isn't claiming the literal truth of her words in relation to my client's clothing, that they were literally soaked in blood." "Indeed, I am," responded McIntyre. "For blood to have stained a garment it must have, in effect, soaked into the material. Hence soaked in blood is entirely accurate."

Judge Clifton pondered the arguments for a moment.

"I'm inclined to side with the prosecution on this one," he announced. "If someone has significant blood on three items of clothing, I think the colloquialism 'soaked in blood' is fair. So, objection overruled."

McIntyre smiled, ever so slightly, then took her time and spoke clearly and methodically to the jury.

"Soaked. In. Blood."

She practically spelled it out now that she'd been given the all clear to use it, letting the phrase hang in the air, to be thought over by the jury.

She paced about as if pondering the words' meaning, letting the silence of the room underscore its significance.

It was classic McIntyre, I'd read an interview with her once where she'd expressed how she liked to identify every case with a hallmark, a memorable phrase that was repeated often throughout the trial, so as to create a vivid image in the jury's mind. And here was one for this trial.

Finally, she turned to Officer O'Reilly.

"And were Alfie Rose's blood-soaked garments sent away for DNA testing, Officer?"

"Yes, they were."

"And what did the results of that analysis show?"

"The results came back with a positive match."

"A positive match for?"

"For the blood of Brian Gates."

It was dramatic McIntyre pause time again, before she turned to address the jury.

"The blood of Brian Gates, was not just merely on the accused, but, in the words of a very experienced officer of the law, 'all over.' That's a significant difference worth noting. Officer O'Reilly, do you think there is another credible reason to explain why Alfie Rose was soaked in the blood of the very man whom he had had a very public feud with, soaked to the extent that it was embedded in the very fabric of his shoes?"

"I don't."

"In your professional opinion, do you believe that it is more credible that Mr. Rose's blood-soaked attire was the result of direct involvement in, and attempted concealment of, the murder of Brian Gates?"

"I do."

She stared at the jury, letting them think long and hard, before finally turning to Officer O'Reilly, almost as an afterthought.

"Thank you, officer. No further questions."

CHAPTER 17

"GRIEF IS a country where it rains and rains but nothing ever grows." The great writer Simon Van Booy said that, and today, of all days, it was truer than ever for me.

Today was August 12, Claire's birthday, at least it would have been if she hadn't been stolen from me. It was a very special day to have been born, and one that we always celebrated together in the same manner, for it coincided with a magical event: the prolific annual meteor shower, the Perseids.

On that night, every year, thousands of shooting stars streak across the sky, the result of the earth passing through the debris trail of a comet's orbit. Those tiny bits of debris, most the size of a grain of sand, become something exquisite when they enter the earth's atmosphere. Traveling at speeds of roughly 130,000mph, they collide with air molecules, exciting a long thin column of atoms along their path as their high level of kinetic energy rapidly ionizes the air, which bursts into brilliance to become what we colloquially know as a shooting star. What a marvel, we used to comment together, that such awe could come from something so tiny and seemingly insignificant.

Every year, Claire and I would get out of Chicago on her birthday, away from all the light pollution to somewhere wild and pure, somewhere we could watch what I would always call her shooting stars.

It was a sacred time, we'd be up together in the middle of the night until the wee hours of the morning, sometimes on a mountainside, other times beside a lake, but always somewhere wild that provided a clear unobstructed view of the night sky, where we could watch the display, arm in arm, while most people were in bed, unaware of the brilliance above them while they slept.

Claire used to call it the world's best kept secret.

And she would always be my shooting star girl.

I hadn't watched those blessed meteors since her murder. I couldn't bring myself to do so alone.

What would be the point?

I knew how it would play out, it would bleed my heart and soul dry to be without her. It wouldn't bring back happy memories; but rather what had happened, and of what I'd lost. And so now, even that sacred night was marred, ruined by the hatred so wantonly cast about by her killer, Alexander. It was always the same, I'd see something good and joyous which would remind me of Claire, and then the images would flash before me: of identifying her defiled body lying on that cold slab in the morgue, and of what I knew must have occurred beforehand, both to her and the tiny children she had tried to protect. It was like black paint poured into a tub of pure brilliant white, leaving a resulting mess of horrible tarnished gray, the two distinct colors intermingled forevermore, now indistinguishable from one other and impossible to separate.

That's what ate me up the most, the desecration of my own memory.

I used to try harder to keep Claire alive there, to preserve my internal image of her, but whenever I did, my own mind attacked her with unwanted thoughts of her murder, overlaying the pure with the grotesque and hideous. I had little control over it, eyes open or closed it didn't matter, and it had gotten progressively worse, to the point where, in desperation, I decided to block Claire out too, lest she drive me insane.

Only today it wasn't working.

I'd been my own worst enemy, and for some stupid reason had watched the documentary Hugh Guthrie had made about the school shooting. I knew it wouldn't do me any good, but like the recovering alcoholic who knows the harm a drink will do to him yet reaches nonetheless for the bottle, I had done the same with the documentary. It was almost a compulsion, but one that brought nothing except misery and pain.

As I sat there watching it in the office, my mind writhed with rage. The footage on the screen on one wall of my office continued to fuel the fire, but like a wild forest burn, I had no way of stopping it.

If I normally managed to keep the rage on a leash, then today it was rampaging free.

Laura was right—someone gave that kid a gun, and they needed to be held responsible for the agony they caused. Alexander had no access to the weapon; his family hated guns and he had no contacts to get the firearm off the black market. He shouldn't have had the gun, plain and simple.

But someone put it in his hands; someone gave him the chance to kill my Claire, and so many innocent children.

My personal philosophy was simple: I didn't believe in an eye for an eye, I believed in two eyes for an eye.

And I thirsted for revenge, not just to hold someone accountable but proper retribution. Hearing eyewitness testimony from those at the scene—teachers, police, first responders—and then the effect the shooting had had on family members of the deceased tore me up inside.

I was angry for myself but also for them. One parent talked movingly of his determination to keep his daughter's light alive, through a foundation he had set up in her name to help disadvantaged children. It was a poignant moment, for I knew that less than a year after the interview had taken place, it had all become too much for the man, and he had killed himself by driving his car off a ravine.

Around the same time, I had also contemplated

suicide. For me, it was like being trapped on the tenth floor of a burning building—the fires that raged in the building, my uncontrolled thoughts, left me no option. The closer the flames came to burning me, the more I looked at the window as a way out. The way I saw it, the way I felt, was the flames were going to kill me eventually, only with a lot more aching to go along with it.

On that night, in the middle of a harsh winter, in the face of another sleepless week, I had to make a choice—face the flames, the indescribable pain of grief, and perhaps die from the burns, or jump out the damn window.

As much as the window was appealing, I chose the flames, and it almost killed me in the process.

I didn't see Casey walk in, but she found me staring, fixated on the screen, with tears in my eyes. I fumbled with the TV remote on spotting her, hitting pause instead of stop, trying in vain to hide what I was watching, for some reason embarrassed as if it were elicit contraband.

"Oh Jack," she said sympathetically, gently taking the TV remote from my hand and putting it down. "Why are you tormenting yourself like this?"

If I'd have known she was coming over I would have held it together, but she caught me unawares, with my defenses down.

She put an arm around me and I let go, sobbing uncontrollably.

You can only bottle it up for so long and although

I was distraught, the release gave me a semblance of peace, albeit briefly.

She fetched me a coffee afterwards and sat down to chat, while I apologized for embarrassing her, which she graciously dismissed.

It was the first time she, or anyone for that matter, had seen me like this, but I guess she always knew.

Most of the time I had my mental and emotional suit of armor on, it was rare that it came off, and, until now, unheard of for me to unburden myself in someone else's presence.

We sat and talked for some time, I can't really remember about what, in a sense it didn't matter, and I felt better afterwards.

But those damn flames were still burning.

CHAPTER 18

AFTER MY moment of vulnerability, I left the office, walked into the nearest bar, took two shots of cheap bourbon, and puffed hard on two cigarettes. It was late, and I very well could've kept going home, but it was still Claire's birthday, and the thought of being alone in my house, only a bottle to comfort me, wasn't appealing. I had already done that too many times.

Walking back into the office with my head down, hopefully avoiding eye contact, I asked Casey what she had. She was sipping on her coffee, feet up on my desk, reviewing notes on her laptop. Me, I much preferred paper files, something solid in my hands, something to hold onto. Who knows where the computer files could go, up into the clouds or the rain or wherever they put those files?

The work I did was sensitive, and security was paramount. A year ago, Casey hired a security expert to look at our systems. Now, when she said security expert, I immediately thought of someone who had done a tour of Afghanistan, all beef and muscle, and was now consulting in civilian life. I expected tattoos, forearms as thick as a tree trunk, and a scar on his face. I expected him to come into the office, beat his fists on the keyboard, grunt twice and then leave.

Turns out, I was wrong. Who would've thought?

The security expert was a former jockey, with the voice to match, and he looked like he struggled to carry his own backpack into the office. Casey told me he was the best, and I let him type with his super-fast fingers on my desktop computer. He was quick, I gave him that, and he really did seem to know what he was doing, but I still kept an eye on my bank accounts for the next month. He could've done anything to my computer, accessed anything, and I would've had no idea how to stop him.

Casey assured me that the expert had upgraded our systems, and our firewalls were rock solid, but there was still something in me that didn't trust the systems enough to upload sensitive documents.

Before she caught me in an emotional mess, Casey had been on her way into the office with new information. I'd initially put her on the trail of Lizzie after what she'd told me about Packman.

It wasn't so much that I didn't believe Lizzie, but I definitely didn't trust her, and wanted to know what she was up to. Casey had staked out her house, but it had been unproductive, Lizzie had only left the house once to go to the shopping mall.

"She's one great flirt," said Casey with a jealous look. "I've never seen someone look more the definition of a cougar than her."

"Cougar?"

"An old lady hunting young boys. That's what they're called. Anyway, the poor eighteen-year-old boy in the kitchenware shop almost had a heart attack. She was rubbing his arm, squeezing her breasts together, playing with her hair, and I swear she rubbed the inside of his leg at one point."

"How'd the boy react?"

"Let's just say that he had to sit down."

"Oh, to be an eighteen-year-old boy again," I smiled.

"I'm sure you don't have any problems there." Casey pushed a strand of hair behind her ear.

"Now, who's the flirt?"

"Sorry." She looked back to the file. "So, I followed her home, and waited outside her house for four hours, but she didn't reappear. I guess she was doing what all cougars do."

I smiled again but didn't bite back this time.

"But a horny young boy and the cougar aren't the big news." She typed into her laptop and my computer pinged with a notification. "I've just sent you a file to review."

"What's it about?" I asked as I slowly, and heavily, punched the keyboard.

As I read the file, it appeared that Casey had had far more luck elsewhere: new information on Packman's business dealings had come to light.

These included a large stock option for one of the production companies he'd penciled in a deal with. It would've kicked in if ratings for the new show were met, and would have been worth a lot of money, but Casey had more.

Much more.

"You look at Packman from the outside and what do you see? Other than an obnoxious bully, of course."

"Success."

"That's right. You see a successful television producer with all the trappings of wealth: big house, flashy car, sailing yacht at DuSable Harbor—nice looking boat too, sixty foot, sleeps six—but when you scratch beneath the surface…"

Casey raised a suggestive eyebrow my way.

I returned one with a smile, beckoning for more information.

"Well, all is not as it might appear. Packman's business dealings are a house of cards, waiting to fall down all around him. To say that they are on shaky ground is an understatement. Behind the scenes he's left a trail of bad investments, so much so that he's on the brink of bankruptcy."

"You're joking. How?"

"Day trading stocks online, badly."

"No."

"Yep. He got into it during the 'dot com' boom of the late nineties. Made some sound, or maybe just lucky, investments back then, and with it made some good money, acquired a taste for it, or more likely an addiction, from thereon in. But things haven't been going according to plan for quite some time. He's bet the wrong way repeatedly and been pummeled by the market, and for huge amounts. Millions at a time. He's been doubling up to try and make good on his losses and taken to using margin—borrowing funds from his broker to buy even more stock, which is all well and good when the market goes his way, but when it turns, he's in twice as much trouble. And trouble, he most certainly is in. The house, the car, the yacht, all remortgaged to the nth degree to try and keep the wolf away from the door. With the loss of income from Gates jumping ship he would have been bankrupted. However, one thing saved him…"

"What?"

"Gates dying."

"How did that help him?"

"Oh, just a little matter of an insurance pay-out on Gates' death."

"Go on."

"Entity redemption plan they call it, where a business purchases separate life insurance policies on its partners—in this case Packman and Gates' joint production company, Alpha Productions. Then, if one of them dies, the business, or remaining partner, as in Packman, benefits from a pay-out."

"That's practically a smoking gun, Packman kills the very person who, had he not died, would have triggered Packman's financial oblivion, but by killing him he averts that financial mess. It's almost poetic, a motive double whammy: revenge and self-preservation in one."

"I thought you might think so."

"And with Lizzie Guthrie, we've got an eyewitness placing Packman at the scene. There's your opportunity too."

"It sure is. If we can somehow get Lizzie Guthrie to testify, then Alfie is off the hook and we've got the son of a gun."

"But how? That's the question."

I was fired up, my melancholy and self-pity evaporated into thin air, replaced now by energy and determination. I was ready for action. We were close, really close, but close wasn't good enough.

Close enough doesn't set people free.

"Casey, I want you back on Lizzie," I said, "We've got to find a way to get her to talk, openly, and on the public record. She's going to be a key in this investigation, and we want her on our side."

"Will do, Jack. I'll get straight on it."

She typed into her laptop again, and my notification went ping. "That's all the files."

"On the computer?" I pointed at the screen.

"Yes, Jack. On the computer." She closed her laptop, picked up her bag and made her way towards the office door, only to double back to where I was sitting.

"And Jack," she said placing her hand on my shoulder. "You have to turn that off," she glanced at the still flickering image on the television screen: an elderly woman standing in the foreground against a backdrop of an upscale suburban street.

In my meltdown, I had forgotten to turn off the television screen, leaving Guthrie's documentary on pause.

"You're right," I said, reaching for the TV remote.

"Wait!" she exclaimed, suddenly turning white.

"What's up? You look like you've seen a ghost."

"What is that?" she said, pointing at the television.

"What's what?"

"That house, what's its relevance to the documentary?"

"It's where the shooter, Alexander, lived. It's his family home. That's a neighbor of the shooter, being interviewed about the kid's unusual personality and obsession with violent video games. Why, what's wrong?"

She paused for a long moment, biting her bottom lip.

"Jack, I remember you saying Hugh was the first person from the media on the scene after the shooting, that he even got there before the cops arrived. You don't think there could be a connection between Hugh Guthrie and Alexander Logan, do you?"

"No, why? I don't understand, what are you getting at Casey?"

"That place, that house," she said, pointing at the house on screen. "I was parked outside of it all morning—it's directly opposite Hugh and Lizzie Guthrie's home."

CHAPTER 19

IT ENDED up being a sleepless night anyway.

As much as I tried to sleep, as much as I tried to keep my eyes shut, my thoughts kept coming back to the documentary of the school shooting.

They had used Claire's photo numerous times on the documentary, the photo where she looked like the innocent angel that she was. That image wouldn't leave my brain, no matter how many times I smashed my head into the pillow. I tossed, I turned, I played with my phone, I read, but nothing could get me to sleep.

The cold, empty bed was the worst. That collection of sheets, blankets and pillows was vast in a way; an ocean of desolate loneliness.

Reaching for someone that wasn't there, looking for someone that was long gone, was as empty a feeling as I've ever experienced.

The missing touch, the absent warmth of another, the longing for something more was bad enough, but it was the silence, that deafening chasm of blankness, that really hurt me.

I couldn't sleep in the bed for a month after Claire

was taken. I would fall asleep on the couch, a large blanket keeping me warm, the sounds of late-night television humming in the background. I often woke to the early morning preachers, and I'm sure some of their words sunk into my mind subliminally. There were days where I felt downright holy, and I seemingly could quote sections of the bible that I had never read.

As the years went by, the nights got better, but there was always a nagging unresolved truth that sat not far from the surface. Some nights were fine, some weeks were okay, some months were manageable, but on the whole, I was missing a lot of sleep.

But even with that pain, it was these nights, the nights when I couldn't turn off the thoughts in my own head, that almost sent me over the edge.

When my phone rang at 6am, I welcomed it, almost jumping with joy for the distraction.

I shouldn't have been so welcoming.

"Jack?"

"Yes."

"It's Betsy-Jane, Alfie's lawyer. We need you, right now. At Alfie's apartment. You have his address?"

"Yes."

"Then get down here as fast as you can," the woman said, abruptly hanging up the phone, not even giving me the chance to reply.

I hadn't expected a call from Betsy Jane, least of all one begging me for help, but that's what occurred in the early hours of the trial's second day.

Alfie's mental state had deteriorated rapidly after his first taste of court, to the extent that his defense team had found him in his penthouse, curled up in the fetal position, rocking back and forth, quietly sobbing to himself, adamant that he would not, could not, go back to face the trial. He was mumbling that he had to get to Mexico, had to run away from it all.

The only person he would talk to was me, and so Betsy made the call.

By 7am, I was outside his penthouse door.

"Come in, Jack," said Betsy, opening up.

"Where is he?" I replied. We both knew this wasn't the time for niceties.

"His bedroom, but before you see him there's something you should know. As well as his Mexico plan, he's been looking at suicide websites, searching for how best to kill himself in a quick and painless manner. We found it in his search history. The pressure's becoming too much for him. And he received an anonymous letter threatening to kill him, from an inmate of the penitentiary he's most likely to be sent to if found guilty. Look Jack, I know we didn't get off on the right foot, you and me, but the plea deal is still on the table. We can get him solitary confinement. He can live through the whole experience. It might be the answer. This might be the only the way he'll live."

It wasn't the right time for me to get into another argument with her, to lay out all the reasons why she was wrong, and the blatant contradictions in her statement.

No, my priority was seeing Alfie.

"I'll talk to him," I said, in a non-committal response.

To be honest, I didn't really know what I was going to say. After all, I was a private investigator, not the kid's parent or counsellor, but he'd asked for me, so I'd agreed to give it a shot. I found him exactly as he'd been described on the phone, curled up in a ball in his bedroom.

"Alfie," I said, reaching out a hand to touch him gently on the shoulder. "We've got to get you out of here. We've got to get you in court, looking fresh. You need to look innocent for the jury."

"I can't do it, Jack. I've had enough. I won't go."

"I know it seems like that. I know it's hard, but it's the only way. If you don't go, they'll arrest you and drag you there in cuffs, and then you won't be home here tonight you'll be in the slammer for breaching the terms of your bail and contempt of court. So that's the choice. It's not, go to court or stay here, it's go to court willingly or get arrested and dragged there."

"What's the point? Why even try? I'm going to be found guilty anyway. I've seen the way the jury looks at me, like I did it, like I killed him. They've already made up their mind, I can see it. I'm going to die in prison."

I recognized the look in his eyes—he was on the tenth floor of his own burning building.

If he was innocent, if he was guiltless, then the thought of prison must've been petrifying. Ten years in prison was paramount to a death sentence for Alfie. I understood his train of thought—why die in there when he could die on the run? If I was facing Alfie's situation, I'd be reacting the same, or perhaps I would've already made a run for the border, knowing what I know about the prison system.

You see, there would be no quick death in prison for Alfie, instead it would be months of mental and physical torment first, breaking his soul into a withering mess, before landing the killer blow. Yep, no doubt, I would be digging my own tunnel to Mexico.

"You can't give up now," I reasoned. "I haven't given up, and you can't either. Look, I didn't want to tell you this and get your hopes up prematurely, but there's a significant development in the case, and I'm working on it. But you need to hang in there so I can do my job. Your job right now is to stay strong; you hear me?"

"What development?" he said, perking up, wiping his eyes with the back of his hand.

"I can't say too much, there's another suspect, and I'm closing in on him. But I can't do that if you crack now. You have to stay strong, especially now."

"You have to tell me what it is, Jack. I have to know."

"We've got someone else in the television industry that was around the dressing room that night. We're looking for evidence that proves it, and we're getting close. We're almost there."

"That's…" He was breathless. "That's amazing."

"Hey, don't have a heart attack on me," I rested my hand on his shoulder. "I don't want to visit you in the hospital again."

"Yes… yes, sir."

A flash of optimism flickered momentarily across his face, so I decided to take advantage with some tough love.

"Man up, Alfie," I said playfully. "Get yourself dressed and get yourself in that court room. On the double, young man!"

He leaped to his feet like a new recruit being yelled at by a drill sergeant, a smile across his face.

I wasn't going to let him jump out the metaphorical window, nor the literal one.

Not when we still had a chance.

CHAPTER 20

DESPITE THE developments in the case and my desire to keep chasing the lead, Alfie had pleaded with me to be in court that morning. He said that he couldn't do it without me there. After a long call to Casey, I agreed to be his support in court, just as importantly, walk him in those courthouse doors, past the crazies that were determined to make a political statement about his case.

Again, I sat in the back row in the courtroom, tucked away from the judging eyes. Everyone who was there had a reason, and there were no fence sitters. They all had an opinion—hang him from the ceiling or release him right away.

"The state calls Dr. Christopher Payne," announced a focused McIntyre when the court had settled in for the morning session.

The good doctor, an eminent looking physician if ever there was one, made his way to the witness stand.

"Would you please tell the jury what you do Dr. Payne?" asked McIntyre.

"I'm the chief medical examiner for district one

and part of district two. I've held this position for a decade and a half and, if good luck would stay on my side, I'll do it for many more."

"For the benefit of the jury, would you explain what a medical examiner does and a little of your background?"

"I'm what's called a forensic pathologist. This means I deal with death of an unexpected and unnatural kind. Instead of disease, I focus on drug overdoses, trauma, shootings, stabbings, road traffic accidents, that sort of thing. And with regards to my background, I first got my degree in 1984 at Oxford University, England, then practiced pathology for five years at Albany Medical Center in New York, then ten years doing forensic pathology for the state of California, after which I took a teaching position in the University of Chicago for five years, and then became a chief medical examiner for the state of Illinois, which I have done for the last fifteen years. I'm certified in clinical, anatomic and forensic pathology."

"Can you give an estimate of the number of autopsies you have performed?"

"It would run into the thousands."

"And does your role involve offering an opinion as to cause and manner of death?"

"Yes, it does."

"I want to take you back to the morning of January the twelfth of this year. Could you tell the court what your professional duties were that morning?"

"I was called to a central location, The Lauderdale Hotel, where a charity event had been held the previous night and a body was found in a dressing room. I entered the premises at around 9:15am and made my initial assessment of the body and its environment."

"What did you find?"

"I found an oddly disturbed crime scene, the body had been dragged from its original location across half of the room, leaving a very clear trail of blood on the beige carpet, indicating its movement from one place to another. And there were blood residues in two locations, a desktop and a table corner. The former of which the head struck, the latter of which it had not."

"Dragging a body like that, would it be easy?"

"Certainly not. The deceased weighed two hundred and forty-three pounds, to be exact, which is a significant weight to attempt to drag across a room. Most people don't realize how difficult it is to move the deadweight of a body. When a person is conscious, even to a small degree, you could say they 'assist,' to a certain extent, in their own movement by another person, by ensuring that their weight is distributed to the other person's core. Whereas the floppy deadweight of a body is very difficult to distribute to your core muscles and, therefore, problematic to move."

"So, it would take a big strong person, to do it?"

said McIntyre, glancing towards six-foot four-inch Alfie.

"Yes, it would, or even two people."

"You mentioned that the deceased's head struck the edge of a table. Could you please give the court your opinion as to the cause and manner in which this occurred?"

"Brian Gates' body displayed two clear signs of trauma: the first was classic blunt trauma to the back of the skull, indicative of a percussive effect from a fixed object, the second was a more serious trauma to the side of the skull, which was cracked in this locality. It is my professional opinion that he was either shoved backwards or punched in the face causing him to fall and hit his head on the table This injury was then followed up with the mortal blow, delivered by a champagne bottle with such force as to kill him. His body was then moved in an inept manner to try and obscure the true cause of death."

McIntyre spent the next fifteen minutes questioning Dr. Payne, getting him to reiterate several times the central objective of her cross-examination, that it would have taken a strong person to move the body, while, oh, look over there ladies and gentlemen of the jury, a big strong man—Alfie Rose. It was simplistic, but straight out of her normal play book, having once remarked in an interview that, to secure a nail, you have to hit it more than once.

I left before the end of the cross examination, it was going around in circles and what's more, I needed space to think. Alfie was running out of time and I needed to formulate a plan; a plan to snare Packman once and for all.

I stood outside deep in thought and lit up a cigarette, inhaling deeply while staring at the cloudless sky. Packman was on my mind, but he wasn't the only one. I tried to focus on him but who was I trying to kid?

There was another presence too, and an unwanted one at that: Alexander, squatting there like he always did, but this time accompanied by another: Hugh Guthrie.

What did their close residential proximity mean? I wondered. Did they know each other, and if so, how well? Thoughts and theories swirled around my head in bewildering complexity but nothing seemed to make any sense.

The phone buzzed in my pocket and I looked at the number.

Laura.

Not this time, old girl, I reasoned with myself.

She would have to wait until I could give her something solid. I was closer than I had ever been, but would that satisfy her? Definitely not.

She rang a second time, and still I ignored it.

When her third attempt to call came through, I conceded.

"Jack." She didn't even give me the chance to answer the phone. "My time is running out and you haven't called me. I can almost hear the clock ticking, it's so loud. I need information, Jack. I need you to solve this."

"Today is a good day, then Laura. I've got something. A connection."

"Between who?"

"Between two people that were there that day. It's an unusual connection, and I'm going to chase it, but right now, I'm due back in court."

"Good." She believed me this time. "Chase that lead. Don't let anything stand in your way."

She hung up the phone without so much as a goodbye. I didn't blame her for the push; if anything, it was what I needed.

I made it back inside the courtroom for the afternoon session, and arrived just in time to catch the last witness of the day: Stuart Craft, the backstage security guard at the charity event, a man who was taking a little too much glee, for my liking, at pointing the finger squarely at Alfie.

He was a funny looking fella: short with stick thin legs but a giant beer gut that flopped over his belt and wobbled like jello, and an oddly creased although shiny-smooth bald head.

Maybe it was to make a point, or maybe he'd just come from work, but instead of normal court attire, he sat in the stand answering questions in his standard-issue black 'security' T-shirt, with said words printed in large letters across the front and back, as if to announce: look at me, I'm a security guard.

"So just to reiterate, Mr. Craft," asked McIntyre

after ten minutes of testimony about his whereabouts on that day. "You began your shift at 3pm and concluded it at 10pm?"

"Yeah, that's right. I finished at 10pm. That's when I went home."

"And you saw the accused, Alfie Rose, enter Brian Gates' dressing room just before the end of your shift?"

"Sure did."

"And what time was that?"

"I'd say about five minutes till ten."

"Did you observe Alfie Rose's manner as he entered the dressing room?"

"His manner?"

"His demeanor or emotional state, whether he looked happy or sad, calm or aggressive, that sort of thing."

"Oh, yeah, I got a good look at his manner, alright. Shifty looking, that's how I would describe him. He looked shifty, like he was up to something, up to no good, and maybe a bit angry too. Yeah, that's right, angry."

I glanced across at Alfie, who by this stage was shaking his head in despair.

It was clear to me that the security guard was embellishing, reveling in his little moment of power over Alfie, but as I looked towards the jury my heart sank: they were lapping it up.

I could imagine the security guard despising Alfie as everything he was not. Alfie was good looking, tall, rich, successful, and had all the girls.

He probably resented Alfie for not having what he deemed a proper job too.

"Playing video games, that's what kids do," he probably thought. "And this big kid is earning millions of dollars, master of his own destiny, while I'm clocking in and out of three jobs, scraping by on slightly above minimum wage."

And so it went for the rest of the security guard's time on the stand, with him painting Alfie the color of the darkest coal, issuing forth little insinuations here and there that made Alfie sound like a man on a mission when he entered Gates' dressing room. And a deadly mission at that.

Sure, Alfie's defense threw in the occasional objection, but the damage was done. And as for their own cross examination, I'd rate it between weak at best, and defeatist at worst.

As the judge dismissed the court for the day, Alfie looked guiltier than ever and nearly as distraught as when I'd seen him first thing in the morning.

I just hoped he wouldn't do anything stupid and irreversible.

Looking at the kid, I decided there and then that this was it, no more trial for me, as much as Alfie needed me here. I had to focus my efforts elsewhere, on pinning Gates' murder on Packman.

Now more than ever, it wasn't just a case I was trying to solve, but a life I was trying to save—and it was currently hanging from a single thread.

CHAPTER 21

THE PUNCH came from out of nowhere, hitting Alfie hard and unexpectedly in the left ear, rocking his head to the other side and nearly sending him to the ground.

He was outside the courthouse when it happened, descending the steps on the way to his waiting car when the mob closed in: journalists, photographers, well-wishers and adversaries; like a swarm of piranhas attacking a carcass, all of them after their own little bit of flesh.

The media in particular was in a feeding frenzy, delighting in Alfie's unprovoked assault; it was good footage for them after all, and that's all they ever cared about.

They were looking at dollar signs, ratings, and copies sold, not an innocent and vulnerable young man on the edge, being pushed, inch by inch, ever closer to it.

Security quickly intervened, dragging away the culprit, a vicious looking miscreant with a face that only a fist could love, leaving Alfie standing there alone, etched with a look of shock and humiliation, but also a haunting embarrassment.

"Don't cry, Alfie!" shouted one of the photographers mockingly, eliciting laughter from his colleagues.

He got what he was after, tears welled in Alfie's eyes as the man gleefully captured the moment.

Rage filled me from head to toe, surging uncontrolled.

A switch had been flipped and I powered towards the cretin.

With an almighty shove I sent him crashing to the ground, smashing his camera into an unsolvable jigsaw puzzle of jagged bits of plastic and mangled electronics.

"Wanna photo of me instead!?" I yelled at him, as he cowered at my feet.

To be fair, his colleagues did; many of them, camera flashes exploding all around me.

And then all hell broke loose.

Punches and kicks flew in all directions, arms and legs everywhere, as others in the crowd began fighting among themselves, while the police quickly circled Alfie and whisked him to the safety of his waiting car.

I didn't stick around.

I'm sure that I'd already made the evening news and I didn't want to add to it. As I walked back to the parking lot, my phone buzzed.

"I've got bad news." It was Casey. "Three pieces of it."

"Hit me with the worst first."

"I can't find anything on Packman. Not a thing that places him anywhere after 10pm that night. I've spent the last eight hours searching for something, even a sniff of a clue, and I haven't got anything. Packman doesn't have a big online presence, and he's not a celebrity, so no-one was taking photos of him. He's the man in the background, the person that no-one pays attention to, and that means there's barely anything about him on the net."

"What about his trash—credit card bills, receipts, or letters?"

"This isn't the nineties, Jack. Most people have moved past the stone tablets that you seem determined to continue using."

She was right. Technology had changed my job a lot in the past decade. People could find out more in an hour with the few clicks of a keyboard, than a week's worth of legwork from the old days. Someone in small town Montana could find out everything there was to know about someone in the middle of London, without ever having to leave the comfort of their chair.

In some ways, that was good, but I did miss the old days. I missed never sitting still, never being in the office, and I hated spending hours behind a screen. That's why I employed Casey as an assistant—she was so much better at computer tracking than I could ever be.

"What about Packman's place?" I asked. "Any chance of getting inside and having a look around?"

"No chance. He's got lots of video surveillance, a tall fence surrounding his yard, and an even taller front gate. You have to be buzzed in just to get past the gate. You could jump the fence, but you wouldn't get far without the security cameras seeing you. It's watertight."

"Any on grounds security?"

"None. It's all electronically controlled."

"And the second bit of bad news?"

"People are starting to post online about their desire to see Alfie killed. There are even threats against him from different accounts."

"And this has been reported to the police?"

"Of course, but all the threats are from anonymous sources, things they can't track. The hatred of Alfie Rose is starting to trend online."

Terrible news, but not unexpected.

"The third piece of bad news?"

She waited a few moments before responding. "I have contacts on the inside, lots of them, and they're all saying the same thing."

She didn't continue, it was obvious what they were saying, but I needed to hear it from her. "What are they saying?"

"Alfie's got a target on his back. As big as they've seen. A lot of credit goes to the long-term prisoners who are able to kill the high-profile ones. There are so many people gunning for Alfie, and they all want him dead. Even the guards are in on the act."

"The guards?"

"The guards in prison don't have a lot to look forward to. Watching Brian Gates on the television was a highlight for them. They adored him, and why wouldn't they? Gates was old school. Someone to look up to. The fact that Gates is gone, the fact that nobody will ever replace him, makes these people angry. And if there's one group of people who don't want to make angry when you're behind bars, it's the guards."

"Thanks Casey."

"What are you going to do, Jack? What's our next step?"

"I'm not sure, but I need some time to think."

I hung up the phone and turned back to look at the courthouse. The people were starting to disperse, going back to their normal lives after expressing their anger at strangers. I'd never been involved in a protest, but I could imagine that once all the energy started going in one direction, once the mob had decided on a viewpoint, it would be hard to stop. Even if you didn't agree with it, it would be hard to challenge the herd.

The walk to the parking lot was another five minutes, and that was more than enough time for my blood to boil.

By the time I reached my car I was incensed, the red mist had descended and my heart pounded hard in my chest. Alfie was being hunted: inside the courtroom, outside the courtroom, in the papers, on TV, even in prison before he was convicted.

The kid didn't stand a chance.

And that's when I decided to go after Packman directly.

To hunt him down right now, this very moment, and force a confession out of him by hook or by crook. No matter what. The decision had been made; I'd get it done now. I was angry alright but determined too.

Failure wasn't an option or Alfie would be dead, maybe even by tonight by his own hand, but almost certainly before the end of the trial by another.

CHAPTER 22

HAVING TRACKED Packman before, I knew where he would most likely be right now, so I wasted no time.

I fired up the engine and hit the gas, driving like a man possessed, weaving in and out of traffic, jumping on the horn, the brakes, the accelerator, in rapid succession as demanded by the road to get there in double quick time until, finally, the tires screeched on the hot asphalt outside Packman's palatial Winnetka home.

It was quite a place: All pillars and ostentatious statues, and more security than Fort Knox.

I was raging inside, but for a second I sat still and tried to formulate a plan, while my heart rate settled down and my breathing became slower.

Two large decorative metal gates stood in my way, blocking access to the property, unless buzzed through by way of a security intercom.

I couldn't imagine that happening so decided on a different approach.

Hitting the gas once more, I tore up the street and spun the car around.

A deep breath filled my lungs as I focused in on my target.

I pulled my seatbelt tight, held on, and dropped the clutch.

The wheels spun, I was thrown back hard in my seat and the car hurtled forwards.

Everything else seemed to disappear; my world became those rapidly approaching gates to the point where it was unclear if I was hurtling towards them or they were headed towards me.

Fifty feet…

Thirty…

Twenty…

Ten…

Suddenly they were upon me, close enough to momentarily see the detail of their filigree metalwork, and then—

Metal split like wooden matches, sparks flew from the door's hinges and the hood and roof of my car, as heavy wrought iron collided hard with the steel battering ram of my beat-up Chevy, now infinitely more so.

The windshield morphed into a thousand pieces that clung together tenuously in one limp fold.

I jumped on the brakes.

The gates clanged loudly as they fell onto the ground, ringing out for several seconds as they rattled to a final halt. And then a strange momentary silence filled the air. There was no time to savor it. I knew it wouldn't last. It was the calm before the storm, and I forecast a big one about to hit.

Jumping out, I quickly surveyed the damage: bumper, hood, windshield, roof, all beyond repair, she'd need decommissioning after this, but I didn't care—I was in.

I ran towards the front door, jumping over little neatly manicured hedges and shrubbery as I went. I knew what I was going to do, what I had to do: I was going in the front door, and it would be by way of my size 13 foot, but when I got within striking distance, my whole game plan changed.

Suddenly the door swung open and there, standing in his jocks with a look of shock and confusion, was Pat Packman.

"What the hell!?" he yelled, eyes darting from me to his mangled gates, then back to me again, his mind trying to catch up with what his eyes were seeing.

I wanted to get a confession, so I gave him a chance.

"I know you killed Brian Gates, Packman! And I know why, too," I yelled, jabbing a finger towards his chest. "You had an insurance policy on your business, and it's the only thing that kept you from bankruptcy, Mr. Record for Violent Assault!"

His surprise deepened, clearly taken aback at what I knew, but then it quickly turned to anger.

He went for me with a punch, swinging wildly.

I slipped to the side, the punch whizzing past close enough to feel the movement of air next to my face.

Now it was my turn, with an almighty lunge I

threw a counter, hitting him with a right hand that could have been fathered by a gorilla.

Packman was a big man, but I'd faced off larger opponents in my time and the shot sent him toppling over into his hallway.

I purposefully hit him high above the jawline so I didn't knock him unconscious: a casualty in the hospital was no good to me, I needed him to talk.

"Admit it Packman!" I shouted grabbing him by the collar and picking him up off the ground, ready to unleash another punch when…

"Freeze or I'll shoot!" shouted a female voice.

I did as instructed, turning slowly in the voice's direction, while tightening my grip around the scruff of Packman's neck.

There, standing at the top of an opulent staircase, was none other than Kelly Holmes in a skimpy negligee, pointing a pistol at my head.

I guess we were both shocked, but then she took a closer look and she was more shocked than I was.

"You!" she exclaimed, recognizing my face from the jazz club.

"You two know each other?" asked a dazed and even more confused Packman.

"You two are together?" I asked, rapidly trying to piece together this odd turn of events.

"What the hell is going on?" asked Kelly Holmes.

It was a good question, and I was wondering as much myself, but continued instead with what I came here for: a confession.

"I'll tell you what's going on, your man here is about to confess to the murder of his former business partner and your ex-husband. A man he killed, for revenge, betrayal and good old-fashioned money."

I tightened my grip around his collar. "Ain't that right, Packman?"

He began to splutter.

"Let him go or I'll kill you!" said Kelly Holmes. "I swear I will."

She was calm but assertive and meant every word.

I reluctantly released my grip on Packman, dropping him onto the floor.

"You're crazy, I never killed Gates," said Packman, rubbing his neck. "I wanted to for so long, but I sure didn't do it."

"Then what were you doing going into his dressing room at the time of the murder?"

"Say what?"

"Yeah, that's right, I've got a witness who places you there at exactly the right time."

"That's impossible," said Kelly. "We were together then and I can prove it."

"How so?"

"We left around ten to go to a restaurant, Everest, on South Financial Place. We stayed there for the next two hours. There'd be video footage to prove it: from the restaurant, from the foyer, from the elevators, loads of places."

"And credit card receipts," chipped in Packman.

"My card," stressed Kelly Holmes, glancing at

Packman, emphasizing whose turn it was to pay next time.

"If that's true, then why didn't you come forward with this information before?" I asked.

"What, and let the whole world know our business? Can you imagine the field day the gossip columnists would have? Ex-wife of Brian Gates, having an open relationship with Brian Gates' producer, whose wife left him for… Brian Gates. No thank you very much. It's our business and nobody else's. And it stays that way," asserted Packman, picking himself off the ground on shaky legs. "Besides, no one was asking, no one but you! No one else is crazy enough to think I had anything to do with it."

"And who exactly are you?" demanded Kelly, turning my way. "As in, who are you really? Because you sure as hell aren't a theater critic."

"Jack Valentine, Private Investigator, working for Alfie Rose."

She slowly lowered the gun.

"Well let me guess, Mr. Valentine," she said. "Your star 'witness,' the one who saw Pat coming out of Brian's dressing room with their own eyes, it wouldn't be a certain… Lizzie Guthrie, now would it?"

I was playing catch up, well and truly on the back foot, so Kelly filled me in, sketching out the details, while I took stock and listened.

"Lizzie was seeing Pat, Pat started seeing me, Pat

broke it off with Lizzie, Lizzie now hates Pat and me," she said. "It's pretty simple really, this is clearly Lizzie's primitive attempt at trying to frame Pat, out of spite for him choosing me over her."

"Let me ask you a question," I said with mock sincerity. "Is there anyone in your industry who is not sleeping with everybody else in it?"

"Very funny," said Packman. "I imagine this comes as a disappointment to you, Mr. Valentine. You thought you had your man, didn't you? Well you don't. I may have made money from Gates dying, but it wasn't me who did the killing."

"If not you, then who?" I said, pondering aloud, more thinking to myself than seriously posing the question, but Kelly offered her assessment.

"What I want to know, is why is no one is going after Lizzie Guthrie? Think about it, she was there at the charity event, she's already demonstrated her willingness to pin the murder on Pat, on an innocent man, and by her own account she visited Brian's dressing room just before he was killed."

She had a point.

I was beginning to wonder exactly the same thing myself.

There was a lot more to Lizzie Guthrie than met the eye. It was time I took a closer look, and quickly.

I turned to leave, to track down Lizzie Guthrie and see where the trail led.

"Hey!" shouted Packman, gazing at the mangled carnage in his driveway. "What about the gates?!"

"The Gates? Oh, yeah…" I replied, bowing my head reverently while placing a hand on my heart. "…May God have mercy upon the man's soul."

CHAPTER 23

"I DIDN'T see that one coming," said Casey, as she drove me towards the upscale tennis club frequented every Thursday morning by Lizzie Guthrie.

"I was certain Packman was our man," continued Casey, "The history of violence, the financial woes solved in a single stroke by Gates' death, the personal and professional betrayal, the jealousy. It was all adding up nicely, or so it seemed. But Kelly Holmes is right, their alibi checks out; it's watertight."

"I hear you," I replied. "But it's not all bad, at least Packman and Kelly Holmes are eliminated from our inquiries. And that's no minor development. It may not be the development we wanted but it's a development, nonetheless. And Lizzie Guthrie is looking more and more like a person of significant interest. So, there's progress and momentum, we've just got to keep moving forwards, keep pushing. And I'm going to push Lizzie Guthrie hard—real hard."

After the incident at the Packman home, Casey had agreed to come and pick me up. My car was barely drivable, but I managed to clunk it down the road before the bumper fell off completely. I worked the phone as I waited for her and was able to get a win.

We drove into the grounds of an exclusive country club on the outskirts of Chicago, a big palatial establishment that was all order and civility. The sort of place that reeked of old money and privilege.

Casey pulled up and parked under one of the lights. The day was turning into evening, and I had a feeling that there was going to be a long night ahead.

"Try not to wreck this one," she said as she handed me the keys to her precious car, a brand-new Mini Cooper.

"I'll do my best, partner," I replied.

It wasn't really my style, of course, I was a Chevy man through and through, but under the circumstances, it would have to do.

As Casey left and hailed a cab to make her way back downtown, I strode on inside, making my way through an elegant arched entrance porch that was proudly lined with multiple coats of arms.

The interior of the club was the height of old-world opulence, with dark, highly polished, cherry wood cabinetry lining much of the walls, and crystal chandeliers sparkling overhead. In the dining rooms, tables were dressed in fine white linen, garnished with vases of freshly cut flowers, and laid in silverware with geometric precision, ready for the sports jacket brigade's luncheon, after a vexing hour on the tennis court, at the pool, golf course, or gym. It was unlike any sport club I'd ever used, but then I didn't make the sort of money Hugh Guthrie did, and Lizzie got to live well. It was a deal that suited them well: Hugh got the trophy bride; Lizzie got the easy life that came with the trappings of Hugh's television cash cow.

I made my way to an outdoor bar area overlooking the lawn tennis courts, where I spotted my target: Lizzie Guthrie, taking her weekly tennis lesson from the resident pro. He was young, in his late twenties, I'd say, olive skinned and of Mediterranean appearance, with a super toned athletic form, and the sort of good looks that made you sick.

By the looks of it, not much tennis was going down under the lights, but this was more than made up for by a large dose of flirting from both parties.

Lizzie was in her element, asking for little tips on her forehand technique, with the pro happy to oblige, correcting her posture with one hand on her arm and another fluctuating between her hip and the small of her back.

I ordered a drink at the bar and waited for her arrival.

We'd agreed to meet after I'd given her a call under the pretense of romantic interest on my part. She said she could meet at 8pm, but only after her tennis lesson. It was all a ruse on my part, of course, but I needed an "in" and Lizzie had been more than receptive to the overture.

My plan was simple, lead her on and then when her defenses were down, hit her with what I knew:

that she'd lied to me and that I could prove it. I was in no mood for her shenanigans, no mood to be messed around with today, but I'd play it cool, at least initially, to see what I could get out of her before I dropped the truth bomb and detonated it squarely in her face.

"Oh, Jack!" she exclaimed, on finally spotting me when the 'lesson' had finished. "You must meet Fernando."

Over they came together, her arm looped through his like he was a fancy handbag to show off at the bar.

"Jack, this is Fernando."

We shook hands.

"He's breathed new life into my ball control."

"Yes, Miss Lizzie has very good control of the balls," said Fernando, in a thick Italian accent.

"I bet she does," I said, raising an eyebrow.

"Her game has come so far in such a short period," continued Fernando. "Miss Lizzie is my favorite partner to play with. She is dominant, has very good stamina, and a nice firm grip."

It was eyebrow time again.

"Tennis is all in the movement of your hips, your core, and Lizzie has very good core muscle control, too… a very tight core."

He looked her up and down with something other than tennis on his mind.

"Oh, thank you Fernando," said Lizzie, plumping up her hair.

"Same time next week, Miss Lizzie?"

"You betcha, Fernando."

He kissed her on both cheeks.

"Ciao, Miss Lizzie."

Her eyes followed him as he strutted away in his little tight shorts, back towards the court where another middle-aged female client was waiting patiently for his services. It was going to be a long night for Fernando, I imagined.

Lizzie turned to me.

"Are you going to get a girl a drink, Jack?"

"Sure. What's your poison?"

"Martini on the rocks."

I made my way to the bar, while Lizzie settled in at a table nearby.

Drink in hand—and a ridiculous dent in my credit card for the privilege—I went and joined her.

"Good to hear you're making progress with your tennis, Lizzie."

"Fernando is a very competent teacher. I recommend him to all my girlfriends."

She took a long sip of her martini and looked me in the eye.

"Are you a sports man, Jack? You've certainly got the physique for it."

"I boxed and wrestled a lot in high school."

"Oh, I can see the appeal of wrestling: the close physical contact, the power play, the fight for control over another, and of course, pinning someone down. Maybe you'll teach me, show me the ropes, so to speak…"

"It's been a while."

"Sure, but I bet you never really lose it, like riding a bike. Do you like to ride, Jack?"

I didn't answer but gave a little laugh to encourage her.

Lizzie's tired euphemisms were already getting tedious, but I went with the flow and indulged her nonetheless. I wanted to hit her with what I knew when she least expected it, so I played along with her game for a little while longer, putting the inevitable on pause for a moment so I could get a feel for who she really was as a person. I didn't like what I saw.

It was time again for me to ask myself if the person sitting in front of me was capable of murder. She was definitely capable of deception and extreme self-interest at the expense of another person, but murder is an abominable thing.

Question was: could she do it?

She continued flirting with me, talking a lot but saying little, at least anything useful, so I decided to bring proceedings to their logical conclusion, to lay my cards on the table and see what sort of hand she was holding.

"What I want to know," said Lizzie, "Is why such a handsome man like yourself is still single?"

"What I want to know, Lizzie…" I leaned in close, letting her know I was about to disclose delicate information, possibly salacious.

She leaned in too, a cheeky flirtatious smile on her face.

"…is why you lied to me?"

The smile faded and silence hung in the air between us as I looked her squarely in the eye.

Finally, she broke the deadlock.

"Lied to you? I'd never lie to you, what do you mean Jack?"

She touched my knee in a sign of fake sincerity.

"The thing is…" I said, pausing briefly, letting the full weight of what I was about to say hang in the air, giving her the full McIntyre treatment, adding impact and gravity to my next play.

"Yes, what is the 'thing'?" she replied, confused and now concerned.

I spoke slowly.

"…You never saw Pat Packman coming out of Brian Gates' dressing room."

I shook my head slowly at her with a look of disappointment.

"It was a lie. And a bold one. And I know why you told it to me too. Packman turned you down. He chose Kelly Holmes over you. It must have been a crushing blow to be turned down for an older woman. And you wanted to bring him down for that slight by setting this attack dog on him as punishment. Well, it didn't work. Packman has got an alibi and a good one. He was with Kelly Holmes and there's video footage to prove it, they were having a romantic meal together."

She looked like she might cry, but for the moment kept it together.

"They looked good together, too. Nice couple," I said, twisting the knife.

"I'm sorry Jack," she said, her voice quivering. "I shouldn't have done it but he hurt me, hurt me badly. I wanted to hurt him back. And you were the easiest way to do it. Hugh told me that you had been looking into Packman, so I knew you'd go after him, especially since he was at the charity event that night too."

"Which, of course, brings me to the more pertinent question: what exactly were you doing in Brian Gates' dressing room after the charity event? Because, from where I'm sitting, it looks mighty likely that it was you who killed him."

"What? No, that's not true!"

"Isn't it? You admit to being there at the right time. You admit to trying to frame another person for the murder. And you admit to having an affair with the deceased. What was it, did Gates break it off with you as well, turn you down for a younger model?"

"No, Jack, it wasn't like that. Brian and I were close, closer than I've ever been with any man. When I left his dressing room, he was alive, I swear it Jack. On my mother's life."

"Your mother's already dead… I know these things, background checks and all."

"I was talking metaphorically. Brian Gates was alive when I left, and I was out of there in minutes. We had a quick chat—of sorts, as Brian was pretty darn drunk, he just kept babbling really—but we arranged to meet in the next few days and that was it."

"And then what did you do?"

"I met up with Hugh."

"Where?"

"Aviary cocktail bar."

"In West Loop?"

"That's the one."

"Good choice," I said, having tracked a target there once myself. "What time did you get there?"

"About eleven. Hugh met me a bit later."

"What time?

"Eleven fifteen, eleven thirty, something like that. He's always late."

"So basically, you have no alibi at all. That gives you plenty of time to have killed Brian Gates and made your way to drink cocktails at a fancy bar with your beloved Hugh."

"Hugh is not my beloved. We're married on paper, but that's where it ends. Without those little blue pills, Hugh isn't even a man. Not a real man anyway, not like Brian Gates. Brian was a man of passion, he understood me, I would never have done anything to hurt him. I felt comfortable with Brian, not just sexually, I could tell Brian all my secrets and he would listen, sympathetically, and give me advice, that's why I went back to him."

"What secrets?"

"All sorts of things."

"Like what?"

"Like my marriage to Hugh. It isn't easy, being his wife, with some of the things he's done."

She trailed off, I could see there was more, something she thought I needed to hear, maybe it would be nothing, but my instincts told me a gentle nudge would reveal it.

"The affairs?" I prompted.

Lizzie flashed me with a look I couldn't interpret, confusion, annoyance, or perhaps fear.

She stared down at the table.

"No, not affairs." Her voice was subdued but I could see she had resigned herself to telling me. "Secrets about Hugh…"

"What secrets?"

"Secrets about his career."

Lizzie paused, as she raised her head to meet my gaze, I saw big tears had welled up in her eyes, and then out it came, words that I did not expect and would shake the very foundations of my world.

"Like he gave that kid the gun," she whispered. "I'm so sorry, Jack."

CHAPTER 24

"WHAT KID? What gun? What are you talking about?" I asked Lizzie, perplexed.

And then she told me, spelling it out with no ambiguity, words that would haunt me from this day forth.

"Hugh gave Alexander Logan the gun that he used in the school shooting." She paused and bit her lip. When she continued, it felt like she was hitting me in the head with a hammer. "If it wasn't for Hugh, the school shooting never would have happened. And your Claire…"

My world shattered.

I sat in a delirious daze, half listening, half somewhere else, unsure of everything.

A strange detachment took over, to the point where I was practically watching myself, removed somehow from the scene as the words being spoken dropped unprocessed into the empty void inside of me.

It was three years since Claire's death. Three years too long.

Every day without her was an eternity.

And here I sat, finally, being told to my face, how her murder had come to pass. I desperately struggled to take it in.

"It was all about his stupid documentary," sobbed Lizzie. "Hugh was researching school shootings for his film and discovered that Alex—Alexander, the mentally unstable kid across the street—had been posting things on social media about shooting his classmates, killing them for what he saw as their bullying behavior towards him."

She wiped tears from her eyes.

"Hugh is a big second amendment rights advocate and has often spoken on air against the demonization of gun owners, and of how, with the right training and education, anyone can become a responsible law-abiding gun owner. And so, he thought he'd prove it. He got to know Alexander: befriended him, gave him odd jobs to do in the yard, mowing the lawn, trimming the hedges, that sort of thing, and then finally offered to show him how to shoot. Hugh said that the kid had never been shown trust in his life and that by doing so it would legitimize Alexander in his own mind as a trustworthy person, but you should have seen that kid's eyes widen when Hugh took him down into the shooting range. He was mesmerized, it was like the firearms were precious jewels or something, like they had a magical charge that wore off on him. It was scary."

I shook my head in despair.

"I voiced my concerns, Jack, really I did, but Hugh

wouldn't listen to me. He said I didn't know what I was talking about, that I was turning into a lefty commie or something, and that I was undermining him professionally. He was convinced his film was going to propel him to the next level—to the level of Brian Gates. He was becoming obsessed with Gates' success and obsessed with his own film project. Over the next month, he taught Alexander how to handle and clean a weapon, and then finally how to shoot: pistols, rifles, semi-automatics, you name it. Hugh said it was empowering Alex, that the act of responsible gunmanship was making him into a model citizen who would now have the confidence to deal with the bullies, to stand up to them in a non-violent manner using his newfound self-esteem alone. He was convinced that you could give a kid a gun, even one with behavioral issues, but that didn't mean they would shoot anyone. And so he did, he gave that gun to Alexander. But Alexander did shoot. He went on his rampage that very same day, killing all those innocent children, all those teachers, and then finally himself."

Lizzie took a deep breath and composed herself.

"I told Brian everything. I unburdened myself to him. I always did and he always listened sympathetically, giving me guidance here and there, little suggestions. But this time he was different, it was different, he said he wanted to go after Hugh, to go after him professionally. He wanted to expose him live on air for what he'd done and take him down once and for all. They never liked each other anyway, but this lit a fire under Brian, and he wouldn't let it drop."

I sat in silence for a moment trying to process everything, while a unifying fury grew inside me, increasing by the second until I felt ready to explode.

Hugh would pay for this, for his lies, his stupidity, his arrogance, his treachery, his deception, but mainly for the murder, the wholly unavoidable murder, of my beloved Claire.

I would get my revenge and Hugh would suffer for it, so help me God. This was my priority, but I couldn't ignore the new information on Gates, it was all falling into place now.

"Talk to me Jack, say something… you're scaring me," said Lizzie.

I took a deep breath, releasing it slowly. I had to show Lizzie that I was calm, that I won't do anything rash.

"What are you going to do?" she asked.

"I need to see him. Talk to him, get closure."

CHAPTER 25

I STOOD outside Hugh's office block and tried desperately to put the rage inside me on hold, to momentarily lower it from the boiling point, if for just a minute, so it wouldn't cloud my judgment and I could formulate a coherent plan.

I'd convinced Lizzie not to call ahead, told her that I needed an honest response from Hugh, not a rehearsed script, that it was the only way I could get closure.

In truth, I wanted to kill Hugh.

I wanted it more than anything.

I needed him to feel my pain, to feel the pain he had caused so many others.

But it wasn't, and I couldn't allow myself to let it be, my only objective.

Nothing I could do would bring back Claire, nothing I could do would help her now, but, if I was smart, I could still help Alfie. If not, he'd be dead too.

And Hugh's fingerprints, it now seemed highly likely, were all over the murder of Brian Gates: the jealousy and obsession with Gates, his wife having an historic and recently rekindled love affair with Gates, and, most importantly of all, the planned takedown of Hugh by Gates himself, that would expose Hugh as the person who supplied the gun used in the school shooting that had taken my beloved Claire from me.

Revenge against Hugh without justice for Alfie—without saving Alfie's life—would be hollow. Hugh would have killed another, only this time I was in a position to stop it, to stop him before it was too late and bring Alfie back from the brink.

"Jack, come on up!" exclaimed an unsuspecting Hugh enthusiastically over the front desk phone on the ground floor.

I handed it back to the receptionist who'd placed the call for me. She pointed me in the right direction, and minutes later, there I was, on the fifth floor, making my way across an expansive shared workspace filled with staff, towards Hugh's secluded personal office on the other side.

I didn't knock.

"Jack, good to see you," he said, as I entered his grandiose office.

It was all decked out to make a statement: that you had just entered the domain of a serious television player. A giant lavish hardwood desk sat center stage like an altar, where subordinates would be expected to make groveling offerings to the great anchorman of conservative news.

The only offering today would be a sacrificial one: Hugh himself.

Behind his altar sat a throne, a ridiculously

oversized red leather office chair, that screamed inadequacies in other departments. Lining the walls were framed pictures of Hugh with the notable guests he'd interviewed over the years, no one A-list of course, he wasn't in that league, but then that was all kind of the point; he wanted to be, wanted people to think he was, and the 'try hard' pretense of his office would have to do in place of true success.

"How are things?" he asked, throwing a big cheesy self-satisfied grin my way, which had me hating him to my core.

"Not good, Hugh," I stated bluntly.

He sat back in his throne, placing his arms arrogantly behind the back of his head.

"Take a seat, Jack," he said, nodding towards a low status chair in front of his desk.

I wasn't falling for that one, so he could look down on me like I was a wayward pupil in the headmaster's office.

"I'll stand."

"Let me guess what's up: Alfie, right? And you've seen the piece I did on camera this morning on the trial?"

I hadn't seen his piece on camera, but I said nothing to dissuade him of his assumption.

"Look Jack, you and I go back, so I think I can speak candidly to you when the situation dictates, and it does now: truth is you're not backing a winner this time. Your client did it. And I think, if you're honest with yourself, you know it too."

"Is that so?"

"It's like the old duck cliché: if it looks like a duck, swims like a duck, and quacks like a duck, then that's probably what it is. And young Alfie is quacking, and quacking good, and about to be served up, Peking style—mmm, real tasty. Alfie looks like the murderer, acts like the murderer, and all the evidence says he's the murderer. So, guess what he is…? And no prizes for this one."

Hugh was enjoying the sound of his own voice, as per normal, typical self-obsessed, second-rate, newsman that he was, so I let him continue digging; digging that cold shallow grave that I was going to bury him in when he was good and done.

"The problem with these gamer nerds is they don't know the fake world from the real world, Jack. And this world has consequences. I know what I'm talking about here, I researched it, remember my documentary?"

"How could I forget."

He got up and took an award from his office shelf.

"Elementary Question: what could have stopped the school shooting that rocked Chicago? — Winner: Best Factual Documentary," he read from the engraving on the plaque. "This would have to be my proudest work. Really got my central thesis across: that sometimes to keep the peace you have to pack a piece."

"Meaning?"

"If teachers had been armed via concealed carry,

then Alexander would have been shot from the get-go. And Alexander was a computer game obsessive type too; they say he spent hours playing an ultra-violent game before going and acting out his sick fantasy. The thing is, Alfie's not that much different. His life is computer games, living in a virtual world with no consequences. He must have killed thousands of make-believe characters, probably saw Gates as one too, and it's only dawning on him now that this isn't a fantasy, that this time he can't press reboot and start again."

Hugh put the award back on the shelf, adjusting it slightly so it was more prominently displayed.

"But then it would suit you for Alfie to be convicted, wouldn't it, Hugh?"

"What does that mean?"

"I mean, if Alfie is convicted, then the person who really killed Brian Gates gets away with it, which is what you've wanted all along, isn't it?"

He hid it well, but I spotted a flicker of panic in his eyes.

"I have no idea what you're talking about. I'm only interested in the truth. That's all any reputable broadcaster is interested in."

"Well, you're certainly not that. And the truth of the matter is right in front of me."

"What…?"

He floundered temporarily, looking for an angle before opting for confused innocence.

"… Me? Have you lost your mind?"

"Far from it. You had the motive and opportunity. I know all about Lizzie's reignited affair with Brian Gates."

"That's not motive, Lizzie and I have an arrangement…"

"Oh, she told me about your loosely defined marriage, but even then, of all the people to go to for affection, the one man who you've always resented, who you've always wanted to be, turns out he was the one man she always wanted to be with. He had the bigger career, the bigger bank balance, and the bigger something else too; what was it that she said to me? 'Even with his bottle of little blue pills, Hugh isn't half the man Brian was.'"

Anger momentarily flashed across Hugh's face.

That one cut him deeply, but he kept it under control, suppressing the impulse to hit back and lose his composure.

"I'm not going to take your bait, Valentine," he said, in response. "You're obviously under a lot of stress and are clutching at straws. It can't be easy after everything you've been through. I feel sorry for you, really I do. But this is nonsense and you need to stop entertaining it."

"How did it go down Hugh, did you see Lizzie going off into Brian's dressing room for a bit of intimate one on one time and decide enough was enough?"

He didn't answer.

"Or maybe Brian had been dropping hints to other

attendees at the event, acting like it was he and Lizzie who were together, not you and her? That sure would get a man angry, a real man anyway. Is that what happened?"

Still no answer.

"Or was he splashing the cash about too much? Rubbing it in your face that he was the bigger player than you, the more successful anchor, letting you know that you were not in his league."

Silence still.

"Or maybe it was one of those gradual things, a slow burn, the realization that Gates could get away with anything, that he could do and say what he wanted and that the network would still back him to the hilt, and that a large section of the public would always love him, regardless. He had virtual immunity. Whereas you, one false step, one errant remark and that would mean your career would be over, your carefully cultivated, although entirely contrived, wholesome conservative image destroyed. Is that what got to you in the end, is that what did it?"

"Oh, come on, this is silly, Alfie did it. Alfie killed Brian Gates. His defense is feeble, pathetic even: that he went to see Gates to make friends with him," Hugh said the last bit in a whiny effeminate voice, then continued in the same vain. "Does he not have any friends? Poor little Alfie. Oh, please be my friend Brian, I'll give you one of my funny hats, let's post a picture of us together on Instagram."

I took a sharp intake of breath.

There it was in plain sight, only Hugh hadn't noticed it.

"Say that again Hugh."

"What?"

"What you just said."

"Let's post a picture on Instagram?"

"Try the part before that."

"What are you talking about?"

He was confused but he wouldn't be for long, it was revelation time.

"You said: 'I'll give you one of my funny hats.'"

"So what? He did. What's the matter, have you not been following the case, Jack? Alfie gave Brian a hat."

"Oh, I've been following alright, and you're correct, he did give him a hat, only, and pay attention to this bit Hugh… the hat wasn't in the photo, and that has never been made public."

Hugh's pupils rapidly dilated, adrenaline coursing through his system.

Fear. Stress. Panic.

It was plain to see. I was planning to trap him, to set him up, and set him up good, but the fool that he was had trapped himself, put himself in checkmate and there was no way out for him. Not this time.

"The only way you could have known that is if you were in Brian's dressing room after Alfie, which means you're the killer. You killed 'The Gates.'"

The game was up and Hugh knew it.

"Very clever, Valentine. Very, very clever. But you're too late, I'll never admit to anything. I'll never admit to saying a single word about a hat, funny or otherwise. It never even happened."

"You won't need to Hugh," I said, pulling out my phone.

I slowly turned the screen to face him, so he could see that his every word was being recorded.

"Saved automatically onto the cloud," I said. "So, don't even think of making for a grab of it, you subhuman, worthless, son of a gun."

I stared a hole through him, gazing into his soul, with unwavering commitment, rage burning inside me as I thought of what this piece of human trash in front of me had done.

Suddenly it flashed in front of me: a scene from my recurring nightmare.

There they were again: small, fragile bodies strewn around the classroom.

Hideous wounds.

Blood smeared around like paint.

And Claire, choking, gasping, dying on the floor, clutching at the lifeless body of a little boy, begging me for help.

I'd waited a long time for this. Finally, it was payback time.

"You should go down for what you did, smashing a man on the head with a champagne bottle, and normally you would, but not this time…"

A mixture of confusion and what looked like relief appeared on Hugh's face—only the relief wouldn't last for long.

"Because killing Brian Gates is the least of your worries right now… have a guess what else I know, Hugh? Go on, have a guess why I'm really here?"

CHAPTER 26

HIS FACE went pale.

The life drained from him as the penny dropped. He didn't wait for confirmation from me.

With a sudden lunge, he reached for his desk drawer, pulling it open with a critical urgency and grabbing a pistol from inside. He pointed it at my chest; not even an untrained monkey could miss from there.

"I didn't mean it to happen, Jack!"

He was nervous, jittery, on edge, and had good reason. As nights go it was pretty bad: getting busted for murder and now, if I got my way, about to become the victim of one.

"I never thought Alexander would shoot anyone. It was all an accident. A tragic, tragic accident. When I think about what happened, those poor kids, your wife… I feel sick, it's just awful. I really thought I could help Alexander."

Hugh took a deep breath and looked at me with a false sincerity I recognized from his news reports. He got up from his desk and began pacing the room, looking around nervously as if there lurked, in places unseen, some threat other than me, waiting to jump out. The fool, no threat greater than me could possibly exist: I was his grim reaper, his death personified, and everything he should fear in its entirety.

"Brian said he was going to expose me—like it was my fault—he would have destroyed everything I worked my whole life for. And why? For ratings, awards, Lizzie…" he spat the words out. "Pushing me down, grinding me into the dirt, so he could climb even further up the ladder. I couldn't allow that to happen!"

He kept pacing and looking around, while I tried to play it cool. I was prepared to die to get him, but I didn't want to die without taking him with me. Getting shot for nothing was not in the plan.

"I don't believe you Hugh," I said coldly. "You see, there's one thing that just doesn't add up in all this."

"What doesn't add up? You got what you wanted Valentine—the truth: I killed that arrogant philanderer Gates and I gave a gun to Alexander. The former deserved everything he got, but you have to believe me, the latter was a mistake."

"No," I said slowly. "It was not a mistake."

"Of course, it was!" he shouted, jabbing towards me with the gun.

"You must take me for a fool, Hugh. The gun used by Alexander had all its markings ground off. It was a ghost. There was no way to track its origin, where it came from, the history of its owners, who it linked back too, which is exactly the way you wanted it. It was no accident, you didn't even let it happen on purpose, you made it happen on purpose."

"No! That's not true!"

"Isn't it? Then how come you arrived on the scene before the cops did, shooting when you got there, only not with a firearm to help the innocent but with a film camera so you could get the exclusive footage you needed for your documentary. I know you always carry—pack a piece to keep the peace, remember? You could have helped those people, those children, my Claire, but you hid behind your camera, staying outside at a safe distance."

Hugh hesitated for a moment, then gave up the charade.

"Like I said, you're very clever, Jack. We have to make the news now; we can't be reactive anymore. We have to be the news." He gestured towards the award on his shelf. "In my industry, in my business, you do what you have to do to win awards. Awards mean respect; respect means more money, and they don't give those things out for free."

"It went down just the way you wanted it, and that warrants a death sentence in my book."

"From where I'm standing, you're in no position to be issuing threats. Take a look, stupid! You're the one staring down the barrel, not me."

His office phone rang.

Hugh glanced towards it momentarily and I seized

the moment.

Grabbing the office chair in front of me, I swung it at Hugh's arm with everything I had. It connected hard, sending the gun flying and Hugh spiraling from the impact.

He let out a yelp.

Time seemed to slow down as the gun clattered into the corner of the room, equidistant between us. It was split second decision time: go for Hugh or the gun? I chose the latter, diving in its direction while Hugh threw himself towards the door.

As my hands gripped hard onto the cold metal surface of the gun, I spun towards Hugh, ready to shoot.

The door slammed shut.

He was out.

But the chase was on.

I burst through the door after him, but the advantage was his. Ahead sprawled the open-plan shared office space, scores of workers per communal desk, some in their own cubicles, with only the select few, the big shots, with their own office.

All eyes were on me, faces mixed with confusion and concern as Hugh zigzagged through the hordes towards the elevators at Olympic pace, and I followed in hot pursuit, gun in hand behind him.

There was no way to put a round in him up here without endangering bystanders, so I powered forwards, my heart racing in my chest and my mouth dry, as I tried to close the gap.

He reached the elevators just as the doors to one were beginning to close. With an almighty leap he jumped inside, the doors enclosing around him as he disappeared from sight behind a protective wall of polished metal.

I cursed into the air.

By the time I reached the elevators he was already a floor below me.

I jabbed rapidly and repeatedly at the button for the other elevator.

Four floors away and moving at an agonizingly slow pace.

I cursed again and glanced around for another way.

There it was: the fire exit stairs.

I ran towards them and burst through the security door with a shoulder barge, setting off a fire alarm linked to it in the process.

The high-pitched wail of the alarm screamed out as I ran down the stairs, taking great strides to clear several steps at a time.

Floor by floor went by as I twisted my way lower, ever lower, towards the ground level.

Suddenly, I burst out into the main reception area and glanced around from side to side, frantically searching for Hugh.

No sign by the main entrance. No sign by the elevators.

Was he still on his way down? I checked the elevator display. It was still going down, heading to the lower basement, the parking lot.

Hugh was going for his car, trying to make a proper break for it.

Just as I was about to chase him, to run back for the stairs, a familiar voice stopped me in my tracks.

"Jack! What's going on?!"

It was Casey, over by the reception desk ready, by the looks of it, to go upstairs and confront Hugh herself.

What was she doing here? There was no time to ask, not now anyway.

"Follow me," I shouted as I headed back towards the stairs.

She did as instructed, Casey following my lead, as we ran down the fire exit stairs, bursting into the dark parking lot below.

A car tore past us, its engine revving hard into the red zone—Guthrie, behind the wheel and getting away.

"Quick!" I yelled, as we scrambled over to Casey's Mini Cooper.

We jumped in.

I fired her up.

The wheels spun in a frenzy.

And we were on his tail.

CHAPTER 27

"DO YOU want to tell me what's going on!?" yelled Casey, as I drove towards the exit barrier—or what was left of it—its broken pieces lying on the ground, having taken a direct hit from Hugh's car on the way out.

I filled Casey in as best I could, about Hugh's confession, not only to Brian's death, but also supplying Alexander with the gun which led to Claire's murder.

I tried to sound calm, but I could see she was worried.

We pulled out onto the street just in time to see Hugh's car disappear around the corner.

Casey held on tight, while I threw her beloved car around like I was in the Indy 500.

She explained she'd had a surprise call from Lizzie, who'd kept the details to herself, but had let Casey know, in no uncertain terms, that she was worried, both for me and what I might do to Hugh.

I raced through the streets, pushing hard to catch Hugh's car ahead, weaving in and out of vehicles, this way and that, one moment gaining ground, then losing it as Hugh pulled away again, the circumstances of traffic and pedestrians giving and then taking away advantage in a second.

Anger propelled me forwards.

I pushed harder still, the Mini's engine screaming for mercy as I rammed it up and down the gears, driving like my life depended on it, and in a sense it did, until finally Hugh was but one car in front of me.

"Easy, Jack! Easy!" yelled Casey, as we overtook the last vehicle in our way and pulled up alongside Hugh.

He glanced my way and for a brief moment our eyes locked.

Fear.

That's what I saw.

He looked scared, terrified even, but I felt no pity.

He should be scared: I was his predator and he was my prey.

It was a primeval law of nature. He was about to be devoured and knew it. There was only one outcome now.

Casey knew what was coming. She grabbed hard onto the door frame, her fingers digging into the molded rubber as she braced herself, ready for the impact to come.

Metal crumpled as I plowed Casey's car into the side of Hugh's, sending him spinning out of control towards a dump truck parked on the side of the road.

He hit it hard, his forward motion coming to an abrupt halt as his car collided with a far heavier and denser immovable object.

Casey and I fared better, but only slightly, bouncing off a parked car and spinning to a standstill in the middle of the road.

No time to wait for the dust to settle.

Adrenaline surged through me as I leapt from the car and sprinted towards Guthrie's wreck of a vehicle, gun drawn ready for retribution. Casey was on my heels, yelling something at me, but by this stage the tunnel vision had set in, all noise had become muffled and I was oblivious to all reason.

I wanted to make him feel my pain by inflicting it on him. And I wanted the last thing he saw on this earth to be me. The man whose life, whose precious love, whose very reason for living, he had stolen for his own selfish ends.

A low guttural moaning emanated from the vehicle.

Hugh had taken a bad hit but was still conscious. His window was shattered, so I reached inside and grabbed at him, rage saturating my being.

Casey was shouting in my ear but everything was a haze. Noise registered but words went unheard.

Hugh's jacket snagged on something, but I kept dragging, ripping it apart and yelling profanity at him as I pulled him, inch by inch, from the vehicle, until finally he slumped onto the ground in a pathetic pile at my feet.

I raised the gun and took aim at his head.

Hugh screwed up his eyes, ready for the end to

come.

And that's when it happened: an image of Claire flashed before me.

Only this one was different.

No longer racked in pain or suffering, but in all her glory: that smile, that decency, compassion and love. I could almost reach out and touch her.

I faltered, hesitated, and as the image faded, Casey's words finally broke through to me.

"Choose hope and life, Jack. Not despair and death."

Police sirens sounded in the distance. They were on their way. It was decision time.

"You know what Claire would want you to do. She wouldn't want you to go to prison. That's where Hugh should go. Don't betray her memory. Honor it."

Her words thundered in my soul, breaking the back of my hatred.

"Please," she said, speaking tenderly. "Put the gun down Jack… for Claire."

Tears welled up in my eyes and I knew that she was right.

I lowered the gun and stepped back as Chicago's finest arrived on the scene.

I placed the gun on the ground, said that I was no threat, and then raised my hands. They cuffed me, of course, and I'd have to go to the station, but it wouldn't last long; not as the truth was about to come out.

I'd done my job.

I'd got my man.

The streets would be safer without Hugh Guthrie on them. He'd be going away for a very long time.

As I was put into the back of a police vehicle, Casey came up next to me.

"You know what, boss?' she said with a glint in her eye. "I think you owe me a new car."

CHAPTER 28

TWO DAYS later, the afternoon sunlight streamed through the scant mottled cloud cover outside Alfie's apartment building, casting long ethereal beams towards the ground, bathing Casey and me in a holy crimson light as we waited for Alfie to arrive.

It seemed fitting, as if symbolizing all that had come to pass and the positivity that now lay ahead. An optimistic future of fresh ideas and ideals awaited, the nights of shrouded darkness were finally now over; for Alfie and for me.

Alfie arrived wearing his trademark hat, with a broad smile on his face, and a lightness in his step that I had yet to witness. He practically skipped up the steps to where we stood.

I was happy for the kid. To see him so joyous gladdened my own heart too.

After all, as a wise man once said: "Happiness is a perfume you cannot pour on others without getting a few drops on yourself."

"Jack, I can't thank you enough!" he said, throwing his arms around me.

I was old school, a firm handshake was my standard operating procedure, so at first it took me by surprise. But to hell with that, all charges had been dropped against the kid, so I responded in kind, putting my arms around him too, if slightly more awkwardly.

"And Casey," he said, moving to her. "Thank you so much, too!"

They hugged it out as well.

It was a grand moment, everything we'd worked for had finally come to fruition. After Guthrie's confession, they dropped the charges against Alfie this morning, and officially charged Guthrie. Alfie was free and had his whole bright future ahead of him to do with whatever he wanted. This time, the system worked.

"It's good to see you so happy," said Casey.

"It's good to feel it for the first time in so very long. It's like I've been given my life back again, given a second chance, and I don't intend to squander it."

To hear such pragmatism and maturity from him was more than encouraging.

That Alfie would rise again from the ashes of Hugh Guthrie's foul work there was no doubt. He'd been through hell and back and come out the other side stronger, and, dare I say it, come out a man as well.

After they arrested Hugh Guthrie for the murder of Brian Gates, and the rumors spread about Hugh's involvement with the school shooting, I took a call from Pat Packman. He complained about his gates again, saying that he was going to send me the bill, but I was too happy to care.

It was what he said next that caught my attention—he was planning to make his own film exposing the process that Guthrie went through to win the award for best documentary.

He was going to expose Guthrie's whole career; running with the idea that Guthrie created situations to have the inside scoop for his television programs. Packman said that he could already feel the awards in his hands.

It was nice, but I didn't really care.

Guthrie was behind bars and would be for a very long time. Whether that was for his involvement in the school shooting, or the murder of Brian Gates, it didn't matter. He was doing time, and he didn't seem like the sort that would thrive on the inside.

In fact, I'd be surprised if he made it through the year.

Like Packman, the media were going to run with the idea that Guthrie was a bad apple, and make an example of him, so that he didn't look reflective of the whole industry. The news business wasn't going to be painted with his dirty brush, and their only choice was to make it look like he was a psychopath who had a hand in the death of those little children at school.

And child killers aren't very popular behind bars.

"You kept your head, when my own defense team

was losing theirs and blaming it on me. You trusted me, when everyone doubted me, but made allowance for their doubting too. You met with triumph and disaster and treated those two imposters just the same. But kept fighting, until victory was in our grasp, until finally, we'd won the game. Jack. Casey. I owe my life to you!" Alfie was emotional and in a poetic mood.

We tried to persuade him that it was nothing, that the truth would always win out, and that it was just what we did, we fought for justice.

He wouldn't hear it, and if I was in his shoes, I probably wouldn't have either.

"So what now, Alfie?" I asked, changing the subject, unaccustomed to so much praise. "What's next for you? Opportunities abound."

"All that time with the threat of going to prison has made me realize that I want to help people. I want to help those less advantaged than me. I was bullied at school and found my own salvation later through computers and technology. I'm going to set up a foundation for other kids suffering from bullying. To help them find themselves and their own salvation, whatever that may be. I want to eradicate bullying, once and for all, on and offline. And I'm going to fight to do it. I'm going to become the face of an anti-bullying campaign."

"That's the spirit," I said, slapping him on the shoulder. "I'm proud of you."

"I want to shine a light that blazes brightly,

radiating far and wide. To stand strong and dedicated to showing what freedom really means and what it can do for the welfare of mankind. I'm going to launch it on Instagram today. As you know, I'm the number ten influencer there, and I'm going to use my influence to bring about a better world for children, to bring awareness to safety and responsible behavior, especially on social media but also out here in the real world."

"Good for you Alfie," said Casey.

"Speaking of which," he replied. "I'd like you two to be my first online advocates, mind if I take a selfie with you?"

He pulled out his phone and selfie stick with an optimistic grin.

I laughed to myself, Jack Valentine taking a selfie for Instagram was not an eventuality I ever thought I'd come to see pass.

"Sure, go right ahead," I said with a smile. "So long as you realize this face is far better suited to radio."

"No arguments there!" said Casey. "But count me in too."

And there we stood, huddled together for our photo.

"Are you ready?" asked Alfie, as we all struck a pose on the screen out in front of us.

"Yeah," I said.

"Me too," said Casey.

"Okay. One. Two…" he stopped at the last

minute, as if a better idea had popped into his head. "Hold on," said Alfie. He reached up, took off his trademark hat and placed it on my head. "There you go. Now that's better."

Click.

Alfie took the picture, immortalizing the three of us together.

He hit upload.

"Congratulations," he said, holding up the screen as it pinged into life on Instagram. "You're both Instagram stars now."

"Thanks Alfie," I said, taking off the hat to hand back to him.

"No, Jack. I'd like you to keep it," he said. "As a memento."

I was touched. "Aww, thanks buddy."

"And Casey. I've got a little something for you too. A bonus for everything you've done for me."

In his hand, Alfie held out and dangled a key, then gestured across the road.

There, with a double coat of showroom wax and polish, was parked a brand-new Mini Cooper in cherry red.

"Try not to break this one," said Alfie, turning to me with a wink. "It's got even more power than the last one."

"He won't get the chance to smash this car," laughed Casey. "It's strictly off limits, Valentine. From now on, you get the bus!"

CHAPTER 29

THE CEMETERY was exactly as I remembered it.

The American flag proudly hung at half-mast over the entrance, blowing gently in the breeze, a symbol of respect for the people that had passed through, and resting behind the tall metal gates were rows of headstones; some weathered, others perfectly maintained, all a symbol of a life lived and loved. The grass was perfectly clipped, the trees were manicured, and the fences were rust-free.

The sun was just sneaking above the horizon, bathing the area in a gentle morning glow, and a light breeze blew from the west.

Despite the gentle stroll through the grounds, my heart rate was accelerating, and the sweat was starting to build under my jacket. I was wearing my best suit, the one that Claire chose for me all those years ago. It was the one she liked the best, and I only ever wore it here.

Stopping at the end of a line of headstones, I wiped my brow, flattened my tie, and smelled the bouquet of flowers in my left hand, ensuring they were arranged flawlessly.

Her favorite were red dahlias. They were the ones that she would stop and smell as we walked, always bringing a smile to her face. We used to take long Sunday afternoon strolls through different neighborhoods, and somehow, she would always find a florist to walk past, and I would always end up buying her flowers to bring home.

She would arrange them to sit on our dining room table, a blast of red for the otherwise plainly decorated room. I complained about the flowers once, said they were too feminine, but somehow, the next week, I ended up buying three bouquets of flowers on our walk. She always had a way with words, a way to make me do whatever she wanted.

After her death, the only time I ever bought flowers was when I came here.

I still remember the first time here so clearly, so vividly, almost as if it were yesterday.

Surrounded by so many people, all the people that Claire's life had touched, I kissed her wooden casket and watched as it was lowered into the earth. Kids were crying, women were weeping, and old men were hugging.

I didn't talk for days after that. I left the funeral without saying a word, I couldn't, and went home locking myself away from the world. It was only once Ben, Claire's brother, came by to check on me, that I opened my mouth again.

I took one more deep breath, blinked back more

tears, and began to walk the path to her headstone.

I told myself I wouldn't cry today. I wasn't going to let her see me cry again.

Not after three years.

I approached her hallowed ground reverently, every footstep delicate, as if blessing the earth like a prayer.

May Love Continue Long Past the Grave.

In Memory of Claire Mary Valentine.
Loved daughter of Andrew and Laura Cooper.
Loved Wife of Jack Valentine.

I couldn't help it, but my lip quivered, and then like a flood, the tears flowed out.

"I told myself I wouldn't cry this time." I knelt down as the tears rolled down my cheeks, placing my hand on the grass in front of the headstone. "I promise I don't cry all the time anymore. I've been strong. I promise, Claire."

I dipped my head, wiped the tears, and then placed the bunch of flowers at the base of the headstone.

"They're red dahlias, this time. Your favorites. They're the most beautiful you could ever hope to see, a really perfect bunch. The florist said that she made them just for you. I made sure that they all smelled perfect, just the way you liked them."

I kissed my index and middle finger and placed them on the gravestone.

"I've missed you. A lot. I still think about you all the time."

My lip quivered again.

"I love you, Claire."

I drew in a deep breath, wiped my eyes again, and moved back to rest my bottom on my heels, kneeling on the ground.

"We finally did it, Claire," I said. "We solved the case. You can finally rest in peace. We found the man that gave Alexander the gun and now he's behind bars. We did it."

Over the next twenty minutes, I told Claire about the case, about Alfie, and about Hugh Guthrie. I told her about Packman and Holmes, about the whole television industry, and I could almost hear her laughter. I told her about the cars I wrecked, and I could see her shaking her head, but with that cheeky grin still on her face. She would've loved it all.

It might sound strange, but our conversations are never a one-way street. I feel like she's still there, still looking up to me with love. I miss our small moments, those moments that have been long forgotten, but here, I feel like they live on.

"I thought I might see you here today." The voice came from behind me.

"Laura." I stood, wiping my eyes with the edge of

the suit sleeve.

"Oh, Jack. Don't hide it. It's ok to cry here."

I stopped wiping my eyes and offered her a smile.

"You did well, Jack. Really well. Claire can rest in peace now. It's all I ever wanted for my only daughter." She placed her own bouquet of flowers down. "And I'll be off to see her soon, too. Not long left for me now."

I reached out and put my arm around her while we stared at the gravestone.

"You make sure you tell her how much I love her when you do."

"I will, but if there's one thing our Claire always knew, it was that."

She looked up, deep into my eyes.

"Now that justice has been done, I finally feel at rest. I'm so proud of you, Jack. We may not have always seen eye to eye, but when needed, you've always pulled through. My Claire was lucky to meet you."

"Thanks."

I had to look away. The statement from the little woman hit me hard, right in the heart.

"She can rest now. We all can."

I knew what she meant.

That sense of peace, that sense of calm, was something that I hadn't known since Claire's death.

I felt settled and a certain acceptance of where I was, thanks to justice. A simple word that meant so much. Truly there can be no peace without it.

Justice was something I knew I would always pursue, wherever it led me and no matter the cost. For with justice came truth, and my truth I realized now, more than ever, was fighting for it, and whoever was currently being denied its blessed sanctity.

"What's next for you, Jack?" asked Laura. "A break, a vacation, some time off?"

"Hardly Laura," I said with a smile. "In fact, a new case has just arrived. And this one is guaranteed to ruffle more than a few feathers."

THE END

AUTHOR'S NOTE:

Thanks so much for reading *Gates of Power*. I hope you enjoyed Jack Valentine's first book.

Thanks to all the people that made this story happen. To all my amazing family and friends, thank you for your inspiration... and your patience!

Extra thanks has to go out to my editor; to my proofreader Jessica, and to Bel, my cover designer.

Writing is a very solitary pursuit, and I love it and feel I was born to do it, but I'm also a social being who loves a good laugh. That's why I mostly write out of co-working spaces. Co-working spaces are officers where freelancers of various disciplines come together to work in a communal office; be they photographers, graphic designers, writers, or the like. Co-working offers a sense of belonging, a place to go and say hello to people, talk about the football, and have a morning coffee with friends.

Co-working wouldn't work for every writer, but for me, it's perfect.

On the other hand, I need time to think before I even put pen to paper. In that stage of the writing process, you'll usually find me by a beach, in the water, or walking through a forest.

I wrote the bulk of this plot while in Chicago; a lot of the ideas for the story were born after I spent the day around the Buckingham Fountain, watching people come and go.

If you enjoyed this book, please leave a positive review. Reviews mean the world to authors.

I've already started the next book in the Jack Valentine series, so keep an eye out for it...

You can find my website at: peteromahoney.com

And if you wish, you can contact me at: peter@peteromahoney.com

Thank you!
Peter O'Mahoney

ALSO BY PETER O'MAHONEY

In the Jack Valentine Series:

Stolen Power

*****

In the Tex Hunter series:

Power and Justice
Faith and Justice
Corrupt Justice
Deadly Justice

*****

In the Bill Harvey Legal Thriller Series:

Redeeming Justice
Will of Justice
Fire and Justice
A Time for Justice
Truth and Justice

Printed in Great Britain
by Amazon